Attack of the Graveyard Ghouls

Look for more books in the Goosebumps Series 2000
by R.L. Stine:

#1 *Cry of the Cat*
#2 *Bride of the Living Dummy*
#3 *Creature Teacher*
#4 *Invasion of the Body Squeezers, Part I*
#5 *Invasion of the Body Squeezers, Part II*
#6 *I Am Your Evil Twin*
#7 *Revenge R Us*
#8 *Fright Camp*
#9 *Are You Terrified Yet?*
#10 *Headless Halloween*

Attack of the Graveyard Ghouls

AN
APPLE
PAPERBACK

SCHOLASTIC INC.
New York Toronto London Auckland Sydney

A PARACHUTE PRESS BOOK

ISBN 0-590-76783-6

Copyright © 1998 by Parachute Press, Inc.
All rights reserved. Published by Scholastic Inc.
APPLE PAPERBACKS and logo are trademarks and/or registered trademarks of Scholastic Inc.
GOOSEBUMPS is a registered trademark
of Parachute Press, Inc.

12 11 10 9 8 7 6 5 4 3 2 1   8 9/9 0 1 2 3/0

Printed in the U.S.A.   40

First Scholastic printing, November 1998

"MY HOMETOWN"

by *Spencer Kassimir*

My name is Spencer Kassimir and I live in a town called Highgrave.

If you lived in Highgrave, you'd know how it got its name. You see, an old graveyard stands high on the hill that overlooks the whole town.

You can see the graveyard from just about anywhere. From Main Street. From my classroom. I can even see it from my bedroom window.

If you live in Highgrave, you can't escape the graveyard.

Even the sunniest days aren't really sunny here. Highgrave Hill casts a deep shadow over the roads, the buildings, the treetops down below.

On clear days, you can look up and see the old gravestones on top of the hill. They gleam like crooked teeth in the tall green grass.

At night, when a moon hangs low over the hill, the graveyard becomes a frightening place. An eerie gray mist clings to the hill. And the gravestones appear to float free.

Yes. The old tombstones seem to float by themselves. To float over the shimmering mist. To float over the town. Over my house at the bottom of Highgrave Hill.

I guess that's why I have the nightmares. . . .

I cleared my throat and lowered the pages of my essay to my side. Reading a paper in front of the whole class makes me really nervous.

My throat felt as dry as sandpaper. And my hands were so wet, they smeared the ink on the pages.

"Very good writing," Mrs. Webster said, nodding. She had her hands clasped tightly on her desk. "Good description, Spencer. Don't you agree, class?"

A few kids muttered yes. My friend Audra Rusinas smiled and flashed me a thumbs-up. Behind her, Frank Foreman yawned really loudly. That caused his pal Buddy Tanner to burst out laughing. A few other kids laughed too.

Mrs. Webster narrowed her eyes at Frank.

Then she turned back to me. "Go on. Read the rest, Spencer."

I glanced up at the big clock, above the chalkboard behind her. "Are you sure there's time?"

The next part of the paper was kind of personal, kind of embarrassing. I knew it would probably give Frank and Buddy a good laugh.

Like the last paper I had to read to the class. I wrote about the only thing in the world that terrifies me — spiders.

Frank and Buddy never let me forget that paper. After I read it, I found a spider in my desk every morning for a month!

"Read until the bell," Mrs. Webster insisted.

I cleared my throat again and started reading. . . .

Some nights I dream about the graveyard ghouls. Everyone in my family dreams about them.

One night, my eight-year-old brother, Jason, woke up screaming. "They're coming to get me! They're coming to get me!" It took a long time to convince Jason it was just a dream.

My little brother and sister, Remy and Charlotte, also have nightmares about the graveyard ghouls.

And I dream that the ghouls rise up from their old graves and float down the hill. They float into the foggy mist on the side of the hill and wait there. Hiding. Waiting for innocent victims to come by.

And then the ghouls swarm around their victims. Sweep around them, wispy as the fog. And pull them up . . . up into the old graves at the top of the hill.

Everyone in Highgrave knows about —

"Very good!" Mrs. Webster interrupted. She clapped her hands enthusiastically. "Very good writing, Spencer!"

Audra flashed me a big smile. Behind her, Frank and Buddy were giggling about something. They slapped each other a high five.

"Do you think you might want to be a writer when you grow up?" Mrs. Webster asked me.

I could feel my face turn hot. "I . . . I don't know," I stammered. "Maybe."

"*Maybe.*" I heard Frank mimic me in a high, shrill voice. Buddy burst out laughing again.

"Frank, would you like to read your paper next?" Mrs. Webster demanded.

Frank's mouth dropped open. "Well . . . it isn't quite finished."

Mrs. Webster leaned over her desk. "What is your essay about?" she asked.

Frank hesitated. Then he finally replied, "I'm not sure."

The whole class broke up laughing. Frank tried to keep a straight face, but he laughed too.

Mrs. Webster shook her head. "I don't think it's funny," she murmured. She turned back to me. "Finish reading your piece, Spencer. Maybe you will inspire Frank."

Frank let out a loud groan.

Mrs. Webster ignored him and motioned for me to read.

Why can't I be *cool* like Frank and Buddy? I asked myself.

They are total goofs. They never do any work at all. They spend the whole day laughing and talking and messing around.

And everyone likes them. Everyone thinks they are the coolest guys in school.

I want to be cool too. I want to make kids laugh. I don't want to be standing up here, having the teacher tell me what a goody-goody I am. Asking me in front of everybody if I want to be a writer.

How totally uncool can you be?

I glanced at Frank. Even though he sat toward the back of the room, I could see him clearly. His head towered over all the others.

Frank is a big, strong, muscular guy.

I'm short and kind of scrawny and I wear glasses.

That's what I am, I thought, a scrawny goody-goody.

I could feel my face growing hot again. I raised the pages in front of my face and continued reading. . . .

Everyone in Highgrave knows about the graveyard ghouls. Some kids told me about them on the day my family moved here.

They said that the dead people buried in the Highgrave graveyard can't rest. They can't rest because the graveyard is up too high.

The dead have become restless, angry ghouls. Rotting and decayed, they climb out of their graves. They cannot sleep. They can only pace the graveyard and look down on the houses below.

At night, their howls and moans float over the town. If you look really closely, you can see the ghouls. You can see them shuffling through the fog that rolls low over the hill.

And if you go up there at night, the ghouls —

The bell rang.

Books slammed shut. Kids cheered.

"Thank you, Spencer. Sorry we couldn't finish. But that was excellent." Mrs. Webster jumped to her feet. "Okay, everyone. That's all for today." She had to shout over the loud voices and scraping chairs.

"But Spencer has given me a really good idea," Mrs. Webster called out.

The room grew quieter.

"Tomorrow, pack a lunch and wear your hiking boots," Mrs. Webster instructed. "Tomorrow, we will all climb up to the graveyard."

"Huh? Why?" someone called out.

The teacher's eyes flashed. "To summon the ghouls," she replied.

2

"What is metamorphosis?" Jason asked.

Dad squinted across the dinner table at him. "Excuse me?"

"What is metamorphosis?" my brother repeated.

Next to him, Remy and Charlotte were poking each other with string beans, having a very wimpy sword fight. Mom was standing across the kitchen, talking on the phone.

I shoved a forkful of mashed potatoes into my mouth — and screamed in pain. "Hot! Too hot!"

Dad reached into the cardboard bucket for another chicken leg. "Metamorphosis? Where did you hear that word, Jason?"

Jason scratched his curly brown hair. He shrugged. "I don't know."

"Well, it means *change*," Dad explained. "Changing from one thing to another."

"You mean like changing your clothes?" Jason asked.

"Remy! Charlotte! Stop playing with your food," Mom called from across the room.

"No," Dad replied, waving the chicken leg in front of him. "Like a caterpillar changing into a butterfly. That's metamorphosis."

"Oh," Jason replied.

"Why did you ask about it?" Dad wondered.

Jason shrugged again. "Beats me."

"He probably heard the word in a cartoon," I suggested.

Jason kicked me hard under the table.

"Ow!" I cried out. "Why did you do that?"

"Just felt like it," he replied.

Remy and Charlotte thought that was funny. They both laughed and then started poking each other with string beans again.

"Stop it! Stop it!" Mom screamed. "String beans are not weapons!"

"Wouldn't it be cool if Duke could change into something else?" Jason asked. He bent down to pet Duke, our black cat. "Maybe Duke could change into a butterfly. That would be metamorphosis, right, Dad?"

Dad didn't get a chance to answer. Remy and Charlotte had dropped their string beans. Now they were tossing handfuls of mashed potatoes at each other.

Dinner can be difficult in my house.

Sometimes you have to duck a lot.

After dinner, Mom and Dad hurried off to a parents' meeting at school. They left me in charge of the three kids. I sat them down in front of the TV and put on a cartoon video. A *long* one.

Then I went up to my room. I tried to call Audra, but the line was busy.

Audra invited me to a dance at the place where she takes dance lessons. I *hate* to dance. In fact, I never dance. Not even by myself in my room.

So I planned to call and tell her I broke my leg or something. *No way* I'd go to a dance with a bunch of kids who really knew how to dance!

I tried her number again. Still busy.

Sighing, I sat on the edge of my bed and stared out the window. It was a cold November night. Gusts of wind rattled the windowpane.

I gazed out at Highgrave Hill. Silvery moonlight made the hill shimmer. All the way up the steep slope, bare, scraggly trees poked up like skeletons.

I pressed my face against the window glass to see to the top of the hill. And I gasped.

Lights!

Flickering flashes of light. Tiny, but so bright they lit up the old tombstones.

My mouth dropped open as I watched the lights, darting, blinking, floating over the graves.

Like ghostly fireflies.

And then the lights faded behind a curtain of fog. The fog shimmered up, over the dark grass, over the bent, scraggly trees. Covering the hill, covering the old graveyard.

And I heard a horrifying moan. Through the windowpane, I heard a long, low moan floating from the hill.

Human and animal at the same time.

So cold. So sad.

So near . . .

The next morning, a raw, damp morning, we all followed Mrs. Webster to the hill.

I lifted my eyes to the sky. No puffy white clouds. No bright patches of blue. No sun. Just a solid slab of gray that stretched as far as I could see.

An icy wind blew down from the hill. The scraggly trees shivered. Their bare limbs waved at us, as if trying to warn us away.

"Listen up, explorers of the past," Mrs. Webster called, gathering us in a circle around her. "Let's see what the old gravestones reveal about our town's history."

I shifted the backpack on my shoulders. I couldn't find my backpack this morning, so I had to borrow Jason's. It was a babyish backpack, bright purple — the same color as Barney! — and way too small for me.

Jason loved it. I knew he'd be really angry if he knew I borrowed it. I planned to get it back home before Jason missed it.

I heard someone hurrying up behind me. But I couldn't move out of the way fast enough. "Cool backpack!" I heard Frank exclaim.

He tugged it down hard with both hands — and I stumbled back into a group of girls.

Frank and Buddy laughed. Some other kids laughed too.

"Is that a toddler's backpack?" Frank demanded.

"It's called My First Backpack!" Buddy declared.

More laughter.

Ha ha.

Ignoring them, I pulled my baseball cap down on my forehead and started to climb the hill, taking long, fast strides.

"Hey — what's your rush?" Audra trotted up beside me. She pointed to the graveyard. "Take your time. They're not going anywhere."

I slowed down. "Hey, how's it going?" I asked. I tried to turn so she couldn't see the babyish purple backpack.

I usually don't care what people think of me. But I care what Audra thinks.

I really like her. She's smart and funny, and she's the prettiest girl in Highgrave Middle School.

Audra has long black hair and beautiful olive skin. But the most amazing thing about her are her eyes. They're light green, flecked with gold.

I always try to act cool around her. That's one reason I won't go to that dance with her. If I did, she'd see what a klutz I am!

"I'm hurrying because I can't wait to check out the graveyard," I lied.

"It's cold up here," Audra said as we reached the broken wooden gate that led into the graveyard. She zipped up her purple satin jacket.

"It's not so bad," I said. I wanted Audra to think I was rugged. So I *unzipped* my jacket.

I stepped past the gate — and saw a spider dangling from the fence.

"Hey!" I cried out. I couldn't help it. I'm *terrified* of spiders.

I kept my eyes on the spider as I walked by it. I wasn't watching where I was going. I stumbled over a broken fence picket — and fell onto a low gravestone.

"Are you okay?" Audra asked.

I let her help me up. "I *told* you I couldn't wait to check out the graves!" I joked.

Mrs. Webster began passing out long sheets of tracing paper and chunks of charcoal. "Collect as many gravestone rubbings as you can," she in-

14

structed. "When we get back to class, we'll read them and see what the old tombstones tell us."

"Oooooh! I'm a ghoul! I'm a graveyard ghoul!" In the next row of graves, Frank staggered around, pretending to haunt a group of girls.

They laughed and wrapped him up in tracing paper.

The girls all think Frank is so cute! Yuck.

"Let's start here," I told Audra.

We held out our papers and charcoal and started rubbing. The wind began to blow harder. It whipped fall leaves from the trees. They whirled in the strong current, then settled at our feet.

Another gust of wind swept dry dirt into my eyes, my nose, my throat. I started to cough.

"William Swift." Audra read the tombstone. "Died on the hanging tree. 1852."

"Do you think he was a murderer or something?" I took a giant step back from the stone.

"He must have been a bad dude," Audra replied thoughtfully.

"Let's find some other stones to rub," I told Audra. I gathered up my supplies and started to wander through the gravestones.

The sky darkened. The air grew colder. I zipped my jacket back up. I shifted the little backpack again and continued to move through the tilted, broken old stones.

I stopped when I found a big grave with a double gravestone.

15

"Oswald Manse. 1770 to 1785. Martin Manse. 1772 to 1785," I read to myself. "Together in life. Together in death."

They were buried under the same stone, I realized. I read the writing again. Oswald Manse was fifteen when he died. Martin was thirteen. They must have been brothers, I realized.

Poor Oswald and Martin Manse. They were so young when they died. I bet they were nice kids. Definitely not murderers who died on the hanging tree! There was some more writing at the bottom of the stone, but I didn't read it.

Beneath the writing, I saw a picture of a bird etched into the granite. It looked like a crow.

I stared at the bird. Audra will like this grave, I thought. She'll want to do a rubbing of it.

Where was Audra, anyway?

I glanced around the graveyard. Kids were scattered everywhere, bending over the graves, struggling with their tracings.

I found Audra with Frank. They were wandering between rows of crooked tombstones, trying to decide which ones to work on next.

"Hey, Audra, check this one out." I grabbed her arm and tugged her to the spot.

"Whoooooah!" I stumbled again.

I grabbed for Audra to keep myself from falling. Missed.

And tumbled forward — *onto the double tombstone!*

16

The stone creaked and groaned as I fell over it.

It toppled over, making a heavy *THUD* as it landed on its back in the dirt.

And I heard a small cry.

The sound sent a shiver down my back.

"Huh? Was that you?" I asked Audra.

She stared down at me. "Excuse me?"

"Wasn't that you? I heard a cry. Wasn't that you?" I repeated.

"No. It wasn't me." Audra shook her head.

"Did you hear it?" I asked.

"Nope."

Did I imagine it? I climbed to my feet and straightened my baseball cap. Then I brushed dirt off the front of my jacket and jeans.

I turned to see Audra staring down at the stone. "Whoa. Spencer, do you see what it says at the bottom?"

I squinted at the small writing engraved under the crow: DISTURB OUR REST AT YOUR OWN PERIL.

Another shiver ran down my back.

Disturb their rest?

Did I just disturb their rest?

"Time to go! Time to go, everyone!" I could hear Mrs. Webster calling from the graveyard gate.

But I stared down at the tombstone I had just knocked over. The crow, lying on the ground.

With a groan, I pulled off the backpack and set it against a tree. Then I bent down and struggled to pull the big stone back up.

"Oh, wow," I muttered.

It weighed a ton. I couldn't budge it.

"Hey — somebody help me!" I called. But they were all heading down the hill. Even Audra.

"Hey! Wait up!" I called after her.

I let go of the big stone, stood up, and took a step toward the gate.

And a hand reached up from the ground — and wrapped itself around my ankle.

I opened my mouth to scream — but only a tiny squeak escaped.

The hand tightened its grip on my ankle. I could feel the cold of its flesh wrap around me.

"Noooooo." I uttered a low moan of horror. And *kicked* hard.

And burst free.

I lurched forward. My baseball cap flew off. I didn't stop to pick it up. I ran.

Ran through the broken gate. "Wait up! Wait up!" I shrieked. "A hand! A hand from a grave!"

Audra, Frank, Buddy, and a few other kids turned to stare at me. "Spencer, what's your problem?" Buddy called.

I spun away from them and stared back into the graveyard.

The hand. The cold, cold hand that had poked up from the dirt — *where was it?*

Where?

No sign of it now.

The graveyard stood silent and still. A tiny brown-and-black chipmunk darted between tilting gravestones. I stood watching it, catching my breath, waiting for my body to stop trembling.

Was it really a hand that grabbed me? The hand of a graveyard ghoul?

Or did my foot get tangled in a vine or weed?

I stared at the tall grass between the gravestones. Nothing moving. Nothing there.

With a sigh, I turned and hurried after the rest of the class. They were halfway down the hill.

Running breathlessly, I caught up to Audra. She eyed me suspiciously. "What's wrong, Spencer? What happened to you?"

"Nothing," I replied. "I just like graveyards. You know. I like the . . . uh . . . atmosphere."

Yeah. Sure.

I hope I never have to go up there again! I told myself.

Little did I know that I'd be back in the graveyard before the night was over. *With no chance of getting out alive.*

5

"**W**here is my backpack?" I heard Jason's shrill voice from down the hall.

I was sitting in front of my computer after dinner, finishing an English paper. Downstairs, I could hear my little brother and sister crying. And I could hear Mom sounding very stern: "I won't talk to you two till you stop crying. Now, stop it! Please!"

I tried to shut out all the noise and concentrate on my homework. But Jason popped his head into my room. "Where is my backpack?" he demanded.

"How should I know?" I lied.

"I need it for tomorrow, and it isn't in my closet," Jason whined.

I stared hard at him. Thinking. Thinking . . .

And I realized where his backpack was. I'd left it up in the graveyard!

"It was right on my shelf!" Jason cried. "And I need it tomorrow morning." His voice was climbing higher and higher.

"Uh . . . I think I know where it is," I confessed.

I shut my eyes. I pictured myself in the graveyard this morning. I set the stupid backpack down against a tree.

When I thought that a hand grabbed my ankle, my baseball cap flew off, I remembered. But I didn't stop to pick it up. I ran out of there as fast as I could. And I forgot all about the backpack too.

Now what?

"Go get it!" Jason demanded angrily. He tried to pull me up by the shoulders. "You're not allowed to borrow my stuff. Go get it, Spencer — or I'm telling!"

I could still hear Remy and Charlotte crying downstairs and Mom screaming at them to stop.

If I tell Mom I took Jason's backpack and left it in the graveyard, she'll *kill* me! I decided.

"No problem," I told my brother. "Calm down. I'll go get it."

Why did I say that? Was I really going to climb up to the Highgrave Cemetery at night?

Did I have a choice?

I sent Jason back to his room so I could think. Then I paced back and forth in my little room, three steps one way, three steps back, my mind racing.

I can't go up there alone, I knew.

Once again, I felt the cold fingers tightening around my ankle.

No. No way I can go to the graveyard alone.

I took a deep breath, picked up the phone, and punched Audra's number. "Could you do me a little favor?" I blurted as soon as she picked up.

"A favor? Who is this? Spencer?"

"Yeah. It's me. Can you come up to the graveyard with me — for just a second? I need to get a couple of things up there."

There was a very long pause on her end. Then, finally, Audra said, "You're joking — right?"

I told Mom and Dad I was going over to Audra's to do homework. Then I slipped out the back door, zipping my jacket against the cold wind that blew down from the hillside.

I tested my flashlight as I trotted through the backyards. It sent an orange circle of light over the frosty grass.

Audra met me at the side of her garage. She wore a heavy down parka, and she had her hair tucked under a wool ski cap.

"Are we really going up to the graveyard to get a baseball cap and a backpack?" she asked, shaking her head.

"I already explained," I said, shining the flashlight in her face. "It's the backpack I *have* to get. I never should have borrowed the stupid thing from Jason in the first place."

We leaned into the wind and began our climb. The tall grass up the hillside was slick from the frosty dew. Audra grabbed my arm and we made our way up slowly.

"Frank called me right after you did," she said.

"Huh? What did *he* want?" I asked.

"He wanted to borrow my history notes. But I told him I was going up to the graveyard with you." Audra laughed. "Frank sounded really surprised."

"Why did you tell him what we were doing?" I demanded.

She shrugged but didn't answer. We stepped around a clump of scraggly, bare trees. Their limbs trembled in the wind, making a soft creaking sound.

"Why did you scream up in the graveyard this morning?" Audra asked. "Tell me the truth this time."

"Huh, me? Scream? I . . . uh . . . thought I saw something."

"You don't believe in those graveyard ghouls you wrote about in your English paper, do you?" Audra's green eyes studied me.

"No way," I muttered.

I gazed up to the top of Highgrave Hill. No

strange flickering lights tonight. No eerie mist. The moon floated low in a clear black sky.

We stopped as we walked through the open gate.

I swept my flashlight over a row of old tombstones. They tilted against each other as if asleep.

I jumped as something leaped out from the bottom of a tall, narrow gravestone.

A rabbit.

Audra laughed. "Spencer — you jumped a mile! It's only a little bunny rabbit."

"Let's grab the backpack and get out of here," I murmured. "I'm pretty sure I left it near that double grave."

A cloud rolled over the moon. I struggled to see as the graveyard darkened. I raised the beam of light and swept it along the rows of graves.

"I wish I brought a flashlight too," Audra whispered. I saw her shiver. "It's so dark up here now."

"Just stick close to me," I said. I felt as frightened as Audra did, but I'd never let her know that.

The wind whistled as it blew through the gnarled, old graveyard trees. The bare limbs shook and creaked. Tall grass brushed against the tilting gravestones, making a *SHUSSSSH SHUSSSSH* sound.

We made our way along a row of low graves. "Oh!" I cried out as my left foot sank into a hole. Pain shot up from my ankle. I rubbed the foot till it stopped hurting.

"I'm okay. Just twisted it a little," I explained.

I climbed a low rise and turned into the next row. And spotted the backpack on the ground, resting against a bent, old tree.

I hurried over to it, kneeled down, and grabbed it with both hands. The dew had frozen on it, spreading a thin layer of frost over the canvas. I brushed it off with one hand.

I could hear Audra breathing hard behind me — loud, rasping breaths.

"What's wrong?" I asked. "Why are you out of breath?"

She didn't reply.

I continued brushing the frost off the backpack. But I stopped when I heard leaves rustling in front of me.

I raised my eyes to the sound. I gazed down the row of tombstones — as someone stepped out quickly from behind a tree.

"Who —?" I uttered.

Too dark to see.

The figure moved toward me, taking long strides.

"Audra!" I cried, finally recognizing her. "What were you doing over there?"

But then a more frightening question burst into my mind: If Audra was over by the tree, *who was breathing so hard behind me?*

With a cry, I spun around.

No one there. No one.

Someone stood breathing hard behind me, I knew. Loud, raspy breaths. So close behind.

If it wasn't Audra, who was it? Where did they go?

A chill ran down my back. The backpack slid out of my hand. I bent to pick it up.

When I stood, Audra had vanished again.

"Audra? What's going on?" I cried.

"Sorry." Her voice rose up from a grassy slope. "I lost you in the dark, Spencer. There is a really awesome gravestone here. You should check it out."

I swung the backpack onto my shoulders. Then I raised the flashlight and aimed it in Audra's direction.

She was bent over a tiny gravestone carved in black. "It's a little baby's grave," she called, her voice muffled in the rush of wind. "And it has a long lullaby engraved on the stone. It ... it's so sad, Spencer."

"That baby probably died a hundred years ago," I muttered. I started over to her, the circle of orange light from the flashlight bouncing off the gravestones. "I found the stupid backpack. We can go, Audra."

"Okay. Just come take a look at this," she called.

Fiddling with the backpack, I started along the row of graves toward her. But the light beam stopped on something on the ground.

My cap! My baseball cap.

I had forgotten all about it.

"All right!" I cried happily.

I bent down. Scooped it off the grass.

And screamed.

Resting snugly inside the cap — a head!

A real human head!

Dark, sunken eyes stared at me. The mouth hung open loosely, revealing black toothless gums.

My stomach heaved. I started to gag.

My hands began to shake, and the head dropped out of the cap. It bounced against my shoe and rolled into the grass.

"A . . . head!" I choked out. Too weak for Audra to hear.

"Spencer, what are you doing?" she called through the darkness.

My stomach heaved again. I could still see those blank, sunken eyes.

"Audra . . . help!" I gasped. "A head. Someone's head in my cap!"

"Huh?" I heard the crunch of leaves. Audra came running over. "I can't hear you, Spencer."

"Look —" I waved the cap in my hand.

"Is that your cap?" she asked, narrowing her eyes at me.

"The head . . . ," I murmured through chattering teeth. "A real head!" I pointed.

She gazed down at the grass. "Where?"

The flashlight trembled in my hand. I struggled to hold the light steady. "There!" I cried.

Holding the sides of her ski cap, Audra squinted into the light. Then she turned back to me. "I don't see anything, Spencer."

I stared down, moving the light in slow circles over the grass. No . . . no . . . no . . .

No head.

Vanished.

But I knew I had seen it. Those cold, sunken eyes stayed in my mind.

"Graveyard ghouls," I murmured. "I . . . I thought it was some kind of legend. You know, a creepy ghost story everyone in town shared. But —"

Audra placed a hand on the shoulder of my coat. "Spencer, take it easy. You're shaking all over."

I opened my mouth to reply — but a sound made me stop.

A scraping, scratching sound, followed by soft thuds.

And then, a voice moaned on the wind, "Spencer . . . give . . . me . . . back . . . my . . . head!"

8

"**N**oooo!"

I screamed. Spun around.

I heard high-pitched laughter. And saw Frank Foreman step into the row of graves. Buddy Tanner followed close behind him, along with two big, beefy guys I recognized from school.

"Well? Give me back my head!" Frank declared. They burst out laughing all over again.

"How long were you standing there?" I choked out. "What are you *doing* here?"

Frank grinned at Audra. "Audra told me you two were coming up here for a picnic. So how come we weren't invited?"

"It's not a picnic," Audra snapped. "I told you not to come, Frank."

"We're leaving now, anyway," I said. I started toward the gate.

Frank moved quickly to block my path. "You sure, Spencer?" he taunted. "You sure you're leaving?"

"Give us a break, guys," Audra pleaded. "You're not funny. It's cold up here and —"

"And there really are ghouls," I blurted out.

I was sorry the moment I said it.

Why did I let that slip? I knew they'd never let me forget it for the rest of my life!

"Ghouls?" Buddy sneered. "Hey, Frank, he really believes that stuff."

"Of course he does," Frank replied, grinning at me. "That's because Spencer *is* a ghoul!"

"Let us go!" I insisted.

But Frank grabbed me by the shoulders. The flashlight fell from my hand. It clattered against a tombstone, hit the ground, and went out.

"Spencer doesn't want to leave," Frank insisted.

"Because he's a ghoul," Buddy added. "He's a graveyard ghoul."

"Spencer is a ghoul," the other two guys repeated.

"Get lost!" I yelled, hoping I sounded brave. I jerked free of Frank's grasp. I grabbed Audra's hand, ready to run.

"Come on, Spencer. You know you don't want to leave," Frank insisted. "You want to stay here, right? With the other ghouls?"

"Leave him alone," Audra demanded.

"Hey — we're just kidding around here," Frank told her. He grabbed me and pinned me against a tree.

"What's the big idea?" I cried, starting to sweat despite the cold.

Then I saw that one of the other guys had a rope — and my legs began to shake.

"What are you going to do?" Audra screamed. "Leave him alone. This isn't funny! Come on, Spencer. Let's get out of here."

Frank pulled me away from the tree and shoved me up against a tall gravestone. I could feel the cold stone through my jacket.

I swung my arm to hit Frank.

But Buddy and another boy grabbed me. They pinned my arms behind me.

I kicked my legs. I tried to yank free, but Frank's friends held on tightly.

"You're going too far!" Audra shrieked. "This isn't a joke, Frank! You can't do this to him!"

Frank laughed.

Audra turned to me. "Don't worry, Spencer. I'm going for help." She spun away from us and vanished through the cemetery gate.

"Let me go!" I yelled, twisting and turning, fighting to free myself.

"Graveyard ghoul. Graveyard ghoul." The boys chanted as they wound the rope around me, tying me tightly to the gravestone.

"Let me go." I kicked out as hard as I could. But that made them pull the rope even tighter.

"Bye, ghooooul!" Frank howled. Then they all raced out of the graveyard and down Highgrave Hill.

This can't be happening! I thought, struggling to free myself.

Tied to a gravestone in Highgrave Cemetery in the middle of the night!

"Wait! Please!" I called to them.

"Don't leave me up here!" My heart pounded in my chest. I felt the gravestone on my back, so cold, so cold . . .

"Please — come back!"

9

Frank, come back! Hey — guys!" I
screamed.

I could hear them laughing as they ran down the
hill.

"Help me! Hey — guys! Don't leave me here!" I
pleaded.

I tugged at the ropes, screaming for help.

A fluttering sound above my head made me
freeze.

I felt a rush of cold air against my face. Another
flutter, and something flickered against my cheek.

Bats!

Dozens of chittering bats. My shouts had scared
them — and sent them flying from the trees.

I tried to duck as they darted low over my head.
I saw flaring red eyes — and felt another rush of
cold wind against my face.

35

Back and forth they swooped, chittering, whistling, their wings fluttering so close.

"Please —" I choked out. "Please —"

Another low swoop. Another flash of tiny red eyes.

And then they vanished into the treetops.

Silence now.

Except for the rapid thudding of my heart.

"Spencer, stay calm," I said out loud. "You're not going to be out here all night. Someone will rescue you. Audra went to get help. She will bring someone. They will be up here really soon."

The bitter wind of Highgrave Hill picked up. It whipped the dead, brittle leaves on the ground. It blew dirt up into my face.

The old trees creaked and groaned.

A long, low moan from nearby made my heart skip a beat.

"Where is Audra?" I asked out loud. "What's taking her so long?"

I peered out over the dark tombstones, searching frantically for her.

Where *is* she? Did she decide to leave me out here? She wouldn't do that.

Would she?

I pushed forward, trying to loosen the rope. It was wound around me tightly, from my shoulders to just below my knees. It pressed my hands tight against my sides.

I heaved my chest forward as hard as I could. But the rope wouldn't give at all.

I twisted and turned my shoulders, trying to loosen it. But it remained taut.

With all my strength, I pushed my hands out. But the rope cut through the skin on my knuckles.

"What's the use?" I fell back against the cold gravestone with a bitter sigh.

I stared out at the old tombstones bathed in the light of the full moon.

"Huh?"

Did a gravestone just shift? Did it tilt to one side?

No. It looked as if it moved. But it didn't, I reassured myself. It's just an illusion, caused by the shimmering light of the moon.

But I blinked hard and stared at it — just to make sure. The tombstone beside it appeared to tilt now!

I heard another long moan, closer this time.

The trees creaked. The wind shook their scraggly, bare limbs.

Another tombstone shifted. With a low creak, it seemed to lean back.

Another eerie moan, so close . . . so close behind me.

"No!" My head began to pound.

I have to get out of here!

I twisted and turned and pushed against the rope.

"Somebody — help me! Get me *out* of here!"

I gasped as a green mist rose up from the creaking, tilting graves. Slowly at first. Then faster. Thicker. Billowing up with a sour, sick smell.

The stench grew stronger as the mist swirled around me. I started to choke. I cried out as it settled on my face, stinging my skin, burning my eyes.

Break free, Spencer, I ordered myself. No matter what it takes!

But before I could start tugging, a hoarse voice echoed through the sickening mist: *"I . . . need . . . your . . . body."*

10

"Huh? Who's there?" I gasped. "Who is it? Frank? Frank — is that you?"

"*I . . . need . . . your . . . body . . .*"

The voice was a croak, more like a cough on the wind. The words so faint — but so chilling.

"Frank?" I cried. "Untie me! Frank? Buddy?"

"*I . . . need . . . your . . . body.*"

"Frank?"

The icy green mist rose up around me. I began to feel so strange. So weak . . .

What is happening to me?

I tried to push against the ropes, but I couldn't raise my arms . . . couldn't tighten my muscles.

My knees buckled.

I struggled to hold my head up. I felt so weak . . . so weak.

"Somebody — help," I choked out, my voice only a whisper now.

"Your body . . . give me your body!"

"No —" I gasped.

But I suddenly felt dizzy. So weak and dizzy.

I felt something press down on my head. Something cold and hard. Like a heavy hand pushing down on my hair.

Pushing . . . pushing *into* my head.

I tried to protest. Tried to cry out.

But my mouth wouldn't open.

And I felt so weak. . . .

The heavy pressure made my forehead throb. My brain felt about to explode!

I . . . I can't think! I realized. I can't think of words. I can't think of *anything*.

It hurts. It hurts so much!

The hard, cold feeling moved down to my chest, down through my arms, my legs.

Squeezing me. Squeezing so tight against my chest now, I could barely breathe.

Can't breathe . . .

Can't think . . .

And then I heard a sharp *RIP*.

Like Velcro tearing.

Like a shirt tearing.

Like *skin* ripping apart.

And I felt myself floating. Floating up, up. Floating free.

Up in the air now. High in the thick green mist.

Through the mist, I struggled to focus. I squinted hard — and saw myself!

Floating in the mist, I stared down *at my own body*, still tied to the tombstone.

I tried to cry out. I tried to shout, to call to my body down below.

But I couldn't make a sound.

How can I be in two places? How can I be up here and down there? I wondered, terrified.

As I floated in the mist, I tried to raise my hands in front of my face.

No hands!

I swirled in the wind trying to glimpse my legs, my feet.

No. Not there!

I'm invisible, I realized to my horror.

I'm me. I'm only my mind! I'm me — floating above my own body.

And then, more horror. I watched helplessly as, down below, my body wiggled its fingers. It stretched out its legs. Then swung its head — *my head!* — from side to side.

Then it blinked.

And smiled.

A smile made with my lips — but not *my* smile. My nostrils flared. And my lips moved in a way that I could never move them. They turned down in the corners, curved into a cold, cruel sneer.

Watching in disbelief from the mist above, I tried to scream. But I couldn't make a sound.

Down below, my head turned. It raised its eyes to me, as if it could see me. *"Good-bye, Spencer,"* it said in *almost* my voice. A little raspy, a little hoarse — but almost my voice.

Huh? Good-bye?

I watched my eyes flash in the moonlight. The sneer on my face deepened.

"You disturbed my rest. Your body is mine now. I've been waiting so long."

"Huh? You rose up from the grave?" I cried. A silent cry. No sound. No sound at all. But I could think. Despite my panic, I could still think.

"Are you a ghoul?" I demanded. "Are you really a graveyard ghoul?"

"Not anymore. Now I am YOU."

He answered me. I was silent, but he heard me. He can hear my thoughts.

"You can't have my body!" I screamed. I tried to float lower. I tried to float back to myself.

But I couldn't move. The heavy mist seemed to hold me in place.

"Do you hear me? You can't have my body!"

"But I DO have it!" the ghoul answered in my voice.

"No!" I wailed. "No!"

And then through the icy mist, I heard another voice in the distance. "He's over there!"

Audra's voice!

"That's where they tied him up!" Her words drifted up Highgrave Hill. I could see her racing up the steep slope. And who was that running behind her? My parents and hers.

"Where — where is he?" I heard my mother cry.

And then I saw Audra point to the tall gravestone where my body was tied.

"Spencer! Spencer!" Mom rushed up to my body. "Are you okay?"

I watched in horror as my head nodded yes.

"Don't worry." Dad started to work at the rope. "We'll have you out of here in no time."

Floating in the mist above, I saw the ghoul's lips — my lips — spread into a grin. A triumphant grin. His eyes — my eyes — grew wide with joy.

The bitter Highgrave Hill wind picked up, pushing me forward, until I floated low over all of them.

"DON'T!" I screamed down at them. "Don't untie him! He's not me! Please — don't untie him!"

12

"He's not me!" I shouted. "Stop! Don't untie him!"

But *they* couldn't hear me. *They* couldn't read my thoughts.

What's going on? I panicked. What has happened to me?

I can see *them*. *I* can hear *them*. Why can't they see or hear me? I wondered as I drifted above them.

Somehow, my mind and my body have separated, I realized. "And I don't have a body anymore," I moaned.

I floated inches above them now. I could have reached out and touched them. But I had no skin to touch them with. No fingers or hands. No body.

No voice . . .

But I can see and I can hear, I told myself. And

45

I can still feel, I realized, as the icy wind picked up and made me shiver.

I haven't lost everything, I tried to convince myself. There's still hope.

I watched as Dad tugged at the ropes tied around my body.

My body stepped free.

Everyone gathered around it. All talking at once, so excited, so worried and upset.

Mom hugged the ghoul in my body. Dad squeezed his shoulder.

My body rubbed its wrists where the rope cut through. Stretched its arms. Bent its knees.

My knees.

"Spencer, are you okay?" Audra asked it.

My eyes stared into hers. "I'm — I'm okay," my body croaked. "Just a little hoarse. From screaming, I guess."

"It's a lucky thing Audra was up here with you," Audra's mother declared.

"Let's hurry home," my mother said. "I want to call Frank Foreman's parents. That boy is in a lot of trouble."

"I don't know why he tied me up," my body said. "Guess he was just showing off." He smiled that smile. The smile that wasn't really mine.

Invisible, I stared down at them helplessly, choked with panic. What am I going to do? I asked myself. I can't let them leave here with *him*!

Think, Spencer!

46

I gazed around the cemetery — and spotted my flashlight on the ground.

I know! I'll pick it up. I'll wave it in front of them. That will get their attention!

Yes!

Riding on the wind, I floated down . . . down.

And reached out for the flashlight.

Grab it. Grab it, Spencer, I ordered myself.

Hurry!

But, no.

No. No . . .

I couldn't pick it up.

I felt myself reaching . . . felt as if I had a hand.

Felt as if it passed right through the flashlight.

I'm air, I realized sadly. I'm nothing but air.

"Let's go home." I saw Dad wrap his arm around my body's shoulders. "It's been a long night."

I watched my body lean into Dad, then begin to walk away.

"STOP!" I wailed. "STOP!"

To my shock, my body stopped. "I almost forgot something," it said. Then it bent down and picked up Jason's backpack. "Can't forget this!"

"It's cold up here." Audra shivered. "Let's go!"

"Wait!" I begged as they walked away. "Listen! He's a ghoul! He's not me!"

The ghoul glanced over his shoulder. He stared into the night air — at me.

47

He can see me, I knew. He has the power to see me floating helplessly here.

A gleeful smile spread over his face.

Audra glanced back too. Her eyes swept over me, then over the gravestones. Then she turned away and led the ghoul in my body down the hill.

"What am I going to do?" I wailed. "I have to warn them. I have to let them know he's not me. I have to get my body back!"

But how?

I'll follow them. That's how. And I'll find a way to get their attention once we get home.

It wasn't a great plan, but it was the only one I had.

I watched them step through the open cemetery gate. I tried to follow. But the wind picked me up and swept me back.

I tried again, struggling to move through the thick mist, the powerful wind.

No.

I felt myself floating back . . . back . . .

Back over the double grave with its toppled tombstone. Back over the granite crow with its terrifying warning underneath: DISTURB OUR REST AT YOUR OWN PERIL.

And then to my horror, I felt myself being dragged down.

Down into darkness. Down into the open grave.

"Noooo!" I screamed. "I'm not dead!"

But the dark earth rose up over me. So cold and hard.

"Please!" I cried out. "Don't bury me. I'm alive! I don't want to die!"

I gathered my strength.

I pushed as hard as I could.

But I couldn't move. And I suddenly felt so tired.

"Stop fighting," I thought I heard a soft whispering voice say. "Give in," it said. "Go to sleep — forever."

Sleep forever, I thought. Yes.

I relaxed.

I stopped struggling. I felt my energy drain away.

Yes . . . sleep forever.

Above me, the wind roared. The trees creaked and rattled in its wake.

I heard a *crack*, the crack of a tree branch. It snapped — and crashed to the ground over the grave.

The sound jolted me. Woke me.

Shocked me to life.

"NOOOOO! I will not give in!" I cried. "I don't want to be buried down here!"

With a burst of strength, I forced myself up . . . up through the dirt.

And out.

Yes!

I could feel the wind again. So fresh and cold.

I floated over the graves. Tossed back, then forward by the gusting winds on the hilltop.

I had no power of my own, I realized.

No power at all.

Without a body, I was helpless. I could go only where the wind carried me.

"I want my body back!" I cried as I tossed on the plunging, swirling currents.

Did that ghoul really plan to take over my life?

Did he plan to be Spencer Kassimir forever?

No, I decided. He's a ghoul. He wanted to use my body to escape the grave.

And now that he has it . . .

Now that he has it, what does he plan to do?

My parents, my brothers and sister — are they in danger?

You're not going to find the answers until you get out of here, I told myself.

But how? HOW?

Whoa. A gust of wind swept me lower.

I saw a flicker of light over a gravestone. Then another. And another.

Small flashes of bright light, flickering over all the gravestones now.

And then dark shapes began to form in the mist. Figures rising up all around me, rising from the graves.

People?

No. Not people.

Shadows of people. Their features pale, almost transparent. Shadows hovering over the graves, staring blankly, lifelessly straight ahead.

Tossed by the wind, I watched in helpless terror

as the figures floated up. I recognized old people and young, with withered skin and sunken eyes. Arms missing. Some of them toothless. Some with hardly any flesh at all.

A young woman drifted over her grave. Patches of blond hair stuck to her skull. She wore a pale pink dress, stained with mud, half-eaten away, crawling with white worms.

A man rose up from his grave. His dark hair slicked down and combed neatly, over a skeletal face with no skin and no eyes. A bug poked its head from one empty eye socket. The man grinned up at me, a hideous, broken-jawed grin.

The shadow of an old woman rose up from her grave — and I gasped. Shiny gray slugs — hundreds of them — clung to the bald spot on the back of her yellowed skull.

She turned slowly and stared up at me with the one eye remaining in her fleshless face.

A man in a rotted black suit drifted up from his grave. He raised his lifeless face and opened his mouth as if tasting the wind.

And then he stared up at me. "You're one of us now," he whispered. He flicked out his tongue, black with decay, and licked his cracked, rutted lips.

"You're a ghoul," he whispered. "You're a graveyard ghoul."

"You're a graveyard ghoul," the old woman repeated, scratching the back of her head.

"Welcome!" the young man rasped. "Welcome to the world of the undead!"

"The legend — it's true!" I gasped. "The ghouls DO climb out of their graves at night! They DO float over the tombstones!"

"Yes. The legend is true," the old woman rasped. "At night we pace the graveyard. We cannot sleep."

"Join us, Spencer. Float over the tombstones with us! You're one of us now. You're a graveyard ghoul!" the man exclaimed.

"I don't want to be a ghoul!" I cried. "I don't want to float over the gravestones! I want my body back!"

"You can't have it back," the man whispered.

"It's gone," the old woman croaked.

"Gone. Gone," all the ghouls chanted as they rose up from their graves. "Your body is gone, Spencer. You're one of us now."

"Nooooo!" I wailed. My cry rose and fell on the wind.

The ugly, grinning ghouls ignored me. As I gaped in horror, they formed a circle. Bony hands grabbed bony hands. And they began to dance.

A dance of the dead.

As the mist faded, the shadowy figures moved in and out of the moonlight. Bending awkwardly, their legs shuffling stiffly. Hideous grins on their broken, decayed faces.

Dancing. Dancing as I floated over them.

And as they danced, I felt myself being drawn to them. Floating toward them. Floating down toward the toppled gravestone. An invisible force pulling me back to the open grave.

"Noooo!" I screamed in protest. "I don't want to

be a ghoul. I don't want to haunt the cemetery. I want my body back. Tell me how to get it back!"

The ghouls stopped their eerie dance.

As soon as they did, I felt the force stop pulling me.

"He wants his body back," the old woman cackled to the others.

"It's gone." The man in the black suit floated out of the circle. He moved toward me. "I told you — your body is gone."

"Gone. Gone," the other ghouls took up the chant.

"I know it's gone," I shouted. "But I'm going to get it back!"

"Gone. Gone," the ghouls droned in hushed tones.

"You'll *never* get it back," the man declared over the ghouls' droning.

"Why not?" I screamed.

"Don't you know who stole your body?" he asked.

"No. I don't."

The ghouls fell silent. No more chanting. They all turned toward the man as he spoke.

"Oswald Manse stole your body," he said. "You knocked over his tombstone. You angered him."

"It was an accident," I said. "I'll make him understand. I'll make him give my body back to me."

"Oswald Manse will never forgive you," the man

whispered. "Oswald Manse is mean. He and his brother were filled with a cruelness so deep, some said they were pure EVIL."

"Oswald Manse and his brother burned down half this town," the old woman croaked. "They set it on fire — for fun. People died. So many people . . ." The old woman's voice trailed off.

"You'll never get your body back from Oswald Manse!" the man declared. "Oswald is too mean to give it back!"

"I will get it back!" I shouted. "I don't care how mean he is! It's my body — not his! There must be some way I can get it back!"

"There is a way. Tell him. Tell him," the old woman murmured.

"How?" I cried. "How can I get it back? Tell me!"

"You must discover how on your own," the man answered.

I tried to get the ghouls to tell me more, but they refused. They took up their slow dance of death.

I stared at them, at their gaunt, lifeless faces. I floated helplessly, watching these shadows of death, watching their ugly, twisted bodies dance — and felt the tug of the force again. It began to pull me back down to the open grave.

I have to get away from this graveyard! I struggled against the strange force. *But how? How am I going to do it without a body . . . ?*

The ghouls continued their silent dance, circling the graves, kicking their stiff legs, hands and arms cracking, raising their skeletal grins to the moon.

I felt myself being pulled down . . . down to the dark, cold grave.

Then, suddenly, a strong wind picked up.

It swept me away from the ghouls' unearthly pull.

The wind carried me high over the gnarled trees and swept me with a rush to the ground.

I felt myself spread over the ground, over the thick carpet of dead leaves. And then I heard the leaves begin to rustle and whisper.

A soft sound at first.

Then louder.

A dry crackling. Moving through the leaves. Closer.

The crackling spread. Grew. And became a roar.

Floating in the leaves, I gazed toward the startling sound.

Listening . . . listening . . .

Until I saw the rats.

They moved in a dark sea of gray, rushing in waves through the leaves around the gravestones. Dozens and dozens of them, skittering over the ground. Whipping the leaves with their scaly tails. Uttering sharp squeals of hunger.

Scrawny, starving rats, searching for food.

Sniffing at the dirt.

Sniffing at the graves of the dead.

Sniffing for prey.

As I stared in horror, I saw a rabbit scamper out from behind a tombstone.

The rats rushed forward.

The rabbit rose up on its hind legs. Froze in fear.

A tidal wave of coarse gray fur surged over the poor creature. It disappeared in the sea of gray.

It happened so fast.

The rats scattered, busily gnawing on their meal of tender, juicy meat.

In seconds, very little was left of the rabbit. Bits of muscle. A puddle of blood. Bones picked clean.

I stared at the stampeding rats, sickened at the sight.

Sickened — and desperate.

I stared at the rats — and knew what I had to do.

15

The rats gathered in small clusters, busily gnawing away at their prey. Ripping at the last shreds of the rabbit with their chiseled teeth.

I need a body, I told myself.

I can't escape this graveyard without a body.

I am only air. I will be forced to float here forever. Or else I will be pulled back down into the grave.

Can I invade a body the way the ghoul invaded mine?

Can I take over another body?

Underneath me, a rat stood by itself, stomach bloated and full of rabbit meat, its red eyes glowing in the dark.

A wave of sickness washed over me.

Am I really thinking of invading that rat's body?

I turned away from the creature. The thought was too frightening, too disgusting.

Spencer, you have to warn your family, I realized. Oswald Manse is mean. Your family could be in danger. And whatever he does — you'll be blamed. He's in your body!

Try! I instructed myself. Try to possess that rat.

It will take you out of here. It will take you to your home.

And then . . .

And then *what?*

Let's take it one step at a time, I decided.

Feeling sick, nearly frozen with fear, I turned back to the bloated rat beneath me.

And dove forward.

As I plunged down, the rat's beady eyes jerked up — as if it could see me.

Its tail twitched.

It turned — as if to run.

Before it could move, I forced myself onto its head.

I remembered how the ghoul had pressed itself down over me. Starting at my head, it had pushed inside. Down. Down . . .

Could I do the same thing to this rat?

I concentrated. Down . . . down . . . through its fur. Through its skin. Into the bloated body.

Tight. It was so tight in here. Tight and hot. I tried to make myself smaller.

Concentrate . . . concentrate.

I could feel the rat twisting and turning. It squirmed. And squealed in terror.

It threw its head from side to side, trying to shake free of me.

I concentrated harder. Fixed my thoughts on burrowing inside. Deeper. Deeper.

The rat thrashed on the ground. It rolled violently, left and right. It shook its body fiercely.

Then the body quaked in a final shudder — and the creature went limp. It slumped to the ground, totally still.

I gazed around me. So hot in here. Hot and wet.

I tried to focus. Everything was a gray blur.

I blinked my eyes. I had eyelids. Real eyelids — attached to a real body!

I let out a cry. "I did it! I'm INSIDE the rat! I took over the rat's body!"

I moved my legs — my four short legs.

Yuck.

I let out a squeal. "I don't want to be a rat. I want to be me."

Don't think about it now, I scolded myself. Don't think about anything but getting home and warning everyone about the evil ghoul.

I turned, still testing my legs.

I took a deep breath — then took off.

I ran through the grass. My whiskers brushed up against the tall blades. The grass tickled me. My stomach rubbed the dirt as I ran.

I'm a rat! I told myself.

I'm smelling the air like a rat. And seeing everything through rat eyes. The wind brushed through my fur. My tail trailed in the air behind me.

A million strange sensations. I tried to ignore them as I scuttled over the grass, out through the graveyard gate.

"Someone — help me. Help me!"

I stopped as I heard a faint voice calling from behind me.

Startled, I perked up my ears.

Was someone calling out to me? Who was calling for help?

I stared into the darkness, struggling to focus my strange new eyes.

No one. No one there.

So I scurried on.

"Help me . . . please . . ." I heard the small voice again.

No time, I thought. I can't go back there.

I turned and trotted down the hill.

What would I find when I returned home? Was Oswald Manse as mean as the ghouls said?

Would I be able to figure out how to get my body back from him?

Or was my body lost to me forever?

16

The dry leaves scraped against my belly as I hurtled down Highgrave Hill toward home. My sharp claws pierced the dirt as I ran.

Running so low to the ground felt strange. The trees, even the blades of grass, towered over me. I felt so small — so defenseless.

But my sense of smell was strong. Too strong. The smell of the dirt stung my nostrils.

I ran and ran.

A night crawler poked its head up from the ground in front of me. I stopped to watch it.

It slithered out of its dark hole and slowly wriggled toward me.

My whiskers twitched as I inhaled its sweet aroma. *Mmmmm.* A fat, juicy worm.

Before I could stop myself, I pounced. I sank my teeth deep into the worm's rubbery skin.

Its sweet juices washed over my tongue. I chewed furiously. Chewed it into pulp, swallowing rapidly.

Then I licked the fur around my mouth to collect the last drop of its dark liquid.

What have I done? I thought in horror. I ate a worm! And I liked it!

With the sweet taste still in my mouth, I started to run again.

I ran quickly, but my short rat legs didn't cover much ground. My lungs burned, but I pushed harder.

Home, home. You're going home. I tried to cheer myself on. But what am I going to do when I get there? I wondered.

How am I going to warn everyone? I'm a *rat*!

Don't think about that now, I told myself, panting. You still have your brain, Spencer. You'll figure it out when you get there.

I scampered over a rotted log. Wet mold clung to my fur. I shook myself hard and kept running.

My heart pounded. My throat burned.

Finally, the ground leveled off. Houses came into view, rising over me like enormous castles.

I stopped to catch my breath. Where am I? I wondered. Down so low, the houses didn't look familiar. The blades of grass were as thick as a jungle. The chitter and hiss of insects were deafening.

I scampered through backyards, staring up at

the dark windows. As I ran, my stomach churned and growled.

I'm hungry again, I realized. In fact, I'm starving.

That big worm didn't fill me up. I have to find food. I have to eat — *now*!

The hunger felt overwhelming. It blocked out all other thoughts.

Find food . . . Find food . . .

I stood up on my hind legs and sniffed, my whiskers twitching.

Yes! My nostrils filled with a strong aroma of food.

Dropping back to all fours, I saw an overturned garbage can, silvery in the moonlight.

Yes! Yes! My stomach churned harder. A thick gob of drool ran from my open mouth.

I plunged through the grass and leaped into the spilled garbage. Yum! Big chunks of hamburger! Old hamburger, already turning green. The delicious odor of the rotting meat made me drool even more.

I grabbed up a big chunk in my front paws and shoved it greedily into my mouth. The decaying meat slid down my tongue. I grabbed another hunk.

A scrabbling sound made me spin around.

I saw two red eyes in front of me. Heard a hiss of warning. Then I felt a hard swipe, a scratching blow across my throat.

I uttered a shrill cry and staggered back.

Another rat! *Two* rats. No. More!

They swarmed over the garbage. Grabbing up chunks of the rotten meat. Chewing. Chewing loudly, gobs of drool running from their mouths.

And as they hungrily devoured the meat, they circled me. Red eyes glowing, they moved in. Chewing, chewing the whole time, they closed in on me.

And raised their claws to fight.

I tried to fight them off. A shrill warning hiss burst from my throat. I raised my claws and thrashed the air.

Two squealing rats jumped me, one from the front, the other from behind.

I felt sharp teeth dig into the fur on my shoulder.

With a squeal, I dodged under them. Pulled back hard and swiped my claws furiously in front of me.

Why are they attacking me? I wondered. I'm a rat. I'm one of them!

Maybe they can sense that I'm different, I thought. Maybe they can tell I'm not exactly like them.

What am I going to do? I wondered. I can't fight them all!

With a shrill cry, a rat leaped for my throat. Claws scraped over my back.

I jumped free. Backed up. Backed up till I couldn't move.

I'm trapped, I realized. Trapped against the back wall of the house.

A line of red eyes glared at me as the rats swarmed in for the kill.

My whole body shuddering, I pressed my back against the stone wall. And saw the cable a few inches to my right.

The slender cable-TV cord. My eyes followed it up along the rain gutter.

The rats were squealing excitedly. Claws scraping the air. Jaws moving up and down beneath glowing eyes.

I made my jump before they attacked. Grabbed the cable with both front claws. Skittered up the cable. Scrambled over the rain gutter to the rooftop.

I landed on the cold shingles with a loud *PLOP*.

My heart pounding, I scrambled to my feet. I didn't glance down. I ran across the roof, up one slanted side, then down the other. To the front of the house.

Then I hid in the wet, leafy gutter. Catching my breath. Listening. Sniffing. All my senses alert.

When I was certain the rats hadn't followed me up, I peered over the side of the gutter. To my surprise, I saw my house on the other side of the street.

Home! My heart thudded joyfully.

I gazed at it, trembling, as if I'd never seen it before.

And then, taking a deep breath, I scuttled down the gutter to the ground. And darted through the wet grass and across the street.

I stopped in the front yard. The house stood in darkness. I raised my eyes to my bedroom window. Dark.

Was the ghoul asleep in my bed?

Was my family okay?

I had to get inside. But how?

I started around the side of the house.

But a tingling feeling made me stop. My fur stood on end. My skin prickled.

DANGER!

All of my senses were warning me — DANGER!

18

My body became a warning system. I knew I should be afraid. But I didn't know why.

I sniffed the night air. Sniffed the strong aroma of an animal approaching.

I sniffed again. Sniffed it coming closer.

My fur stood up straight. I heard footsteps. Rapid footsteps, advancing quickly.

I jerked my head around. My ears twitched as the footsteps grew louder.

I stared into the darkness — and I saw him.

First I saw his eyes. Large green eyes glowing like headlights in the dark.

Then I saw his whiskered face. His slender trunk. His paws, moving so stealthily over the grass.

A cat.

Duke. Our black cat.

I let out a sigh of relief. Duke wouldn't hurt me.

Duke trained his green eyes on me. He arched his back.

But I'm not me, I remembered. I'm a rat.

My whiskers twitched. My body trembled.

Duke's fur stood straight up. His lips curled back. He uttered a shrill cry — and pounced.

I tried to dart away, but he was too fast.

His claws closed around me. He pinned me to the ground.

I shrieked as his claws dug deep beneath my fur.

Duke held me down. He leaned over me. I could feel his hot breath on my fur.

I tried to wriggle free, but I couldn't move.

"Duke — it's me! It's Spencer!" I tried to scream.

But only tiny squeaks came out.

And then the cat lowered his head.

I stared up helplessly as his jaws swung open.

His teeth clamped down. Clamped down. Clamped down.

The sharp teeth dug into my chest.

And then slid down my body and dug into my fleshy tail.

Whoooa.

The cat lifted me off the ground. And holding

my tail in his teeth, began swinging me . . . swinging me back and forth.

The ground tilted up. The black sky swept down. The cat swung me wildly.

This is it, I thought. I'm going to die in a rat's body, chewed to death by my own cat.

19

Noooo . . .

I felt myself swinging . . . swinging upside down.

I struggled to focus.

I'm not going to die like this, I told myself. I won't let it happen.

"*Eeee eeee eeeeh.*" I squealed in panic as the cat swung me hard. My tail throbbed with pain. The pain shot up my body.

Another hard swing.

I shot out both front paws.

And grabbed the fur on the back of the cat's neck. With a loud groan, I dug my claws deep into his fur. Held on tight.

The startled cat shot open his mouth.

My tail slid out from between his teeth.

Gripping the cat's fur, I hoisted myself onto his back.

Duke howled in protest. Arched his back. Rose up on his hind legs.

Bouncing on the cat's writhing, tossing back, I held on.

And pulled myself up to his head.

I knew what I wanted to do. But could I hold on long enough?

The cat yowled and tossed his head.

Holding on tightly, I shut my eyes. And pushed. Pushed down . . . down into deep darkness.

Duke's furious yowling seemed to surround me. I plunged deeper, deeper into the sound.

Down . . .

Down . . .

And when I opened my eyes, I stared down at the rat.

Yes. I stared down at the rat, sprawled on its side, dead on the grass.

I tossed my head back and let out a long *meeeeow*. Then I bent down and picked the dead rat up in my teeth. I carried the rat to the back of the house and dropped it beside the kitchen door.

Sorry, Duke, I thought. Sorry to push you out of your body like that, boy. But I need it more than you do.

There are lives at stake. *Many* lives at stake.

I lowered my head and bumped open the little cat door.

Wow! I stood in the kitchen with all its familiar smells. So warm and clean.

I gazed around, purring, so happy to be back here. My eyes swept over the sink, the kitchen table, the refrigerator. I spotted my homework assignment on the kitchen counter.

Yesssss!

So warm and cozy in here, I felt like curling up in my basket near the radiator. I yawned and stretched.

No. No time, I reminded myself.

There's a ghoul in this house. In *my* body.

Shaking away my sleepiness, I padded through the hall. Then I took the stairs two at a time.

I charged through Mom and Dad's open bedroom door. I jumped onto the foot of their bed.

They lay sound asleep, blankets pulled up to their chins. Dad snored softly. Long strands of Mom's dark hair had fallen over her face.

"Wake up!" I pawed Mom. "Wake up! Listen to me! Come on — wake up!"

Mom groaned and rolled onto her side, turning her back to me.

"Dad!" I cried. "Wake up! Come on!"

Dad made a gurgling sound. His eyes popped open. He sat up, blinking hard. "Huh? Duke?"

"What's wrong, dear?" Mom asked sleepily. She lifted her head off the pillow and squinted at me.

"The cat woke me up," Dad replied.

"It's me — Spencer!" I exclaimed. "Can you understand me? Please — listen! There's no time! There's a ghoul in this house! An evil ghoul! We've got to act fast!"

Mom and Dad stared at me as I explained. Then they exchanged worried glances.

"You understand me!" I cried happily. "Yes! You understand me!"

"Why is the cat yowling like that?" Dad asked.

20

"No! Listen to me!" I screamed. "Listen to me!"

But I knew my words were coming out as cat cries.

Mom pulled a pillow over her head. "Get rid of him," she moaned. "I can't stand that screeching."

"Let's go, Duke," Dad said. He sat up and made a grab for me.

I leaped to the floor. My mind whirred frantically. How can I let them know it's me? How can I make them listen?

I saw Mom's notebook open on the desk by the window. And a pen lying beside the notebook.

I'll *write* a message! I decided.

I saw Dad climb out of bed. "Come on, Duke," he sighed sleepily. "Don't try to run away. You have to go back outside."

I turned away from him and jumped onto the desk. I stabbed my claws out and grabbed the pen. It rolled out from under my paw.

I tried again.

No. No way.

No way to grip it.

I lowered my head and tried to pick the pen up in my mouth. But it rolled off the desktop onto the bedroom carpet.

Before I could go after it, Dad wrapped his hands around me. "Dumb cat. It's a little late to be playing with pens."

I struggled and squirmed and yowled my head off. But Dad carried me downstairs and tossed me out the back door.

The door slammed behind me.

It took me a few seconds to gain my balance. I still wasn't used to walking on all fours. Then I charged back up to the cat door. I lowered my head and pushed.

Ouch!

Dad had locked the cat door.

Okay. No problem, I thought. I'm a cat. I'll climb in through a window.

I scampered up the tree at the back of the house. Then I carefully made my way along the branch outside my bedroom window.

Taking a deep breath, I arched my back — and leaped onto the window ledge.

The window was open a few inches. Was the

ghoul in my body asleep in my bed? The billowing curtains blocked my view.

I flattened myself on the narrow ledge. A tight squeeze, I saw. But cats can squeeze through anything — right?

I poked my head into the bedroom. Flattened myself. Flattened myself . . .

Squeezed through the window and crawled into the room.

The curtains fluttered around me. I dropped silently to the floor. Crossed the room to my bed.

Then I hopped onto the foot of the bed — and gasped.

21

The pillows had been ripped apart. Feathers and stuffing covered the bed, the floor, my dresser.

The sheets were also ripped. Torn into thin strips. The mattress had a gaping hole in its center.

In the light from the window, I saw that my closet door had been pulled off its hinges. It stood tilted against the wall. My clothes had been pulled off the closet shelves, tossed on the floor.

The wallpaper beside my dresser was shredded. It looked as if it had been clawed off the wall.

"He really is evil!" I gasped. "He's — he's a monster!"

But where is he?

Then I heard a clattering sound. A soft *THUD*. From downstairs.

I spun toward the door. Creeping into the hall, I followed the sounds, down to the kitchen.

And there he stood. There *I* stood, in the glow of the refrigerator.

I walked silently into the kitchen. He didn't see me. He was too busy stuffing his face.

Leaning into the refrigerator, he jammed handfuls of food into his mouth.

Staring in shock, I watched him open a jar of pickles and swallow them all whole. He tossed the jar to the floor.

Then he started grabbing up raw eggs from the refrigerator door and slamming them into his mouth.

He smashed a Coke bottle on the side of the refrigerator, tilted his head back, and drank the liquid down in a gulp. Then he tossed the bottle across the kitchen and stuffed a whole head of lettuce into his mouth.

I took a few steps closer, into the square of refrigerator light.

The ghoul tilted a jar of mayonnaise to his mouth and hungrily gulped it down. He was still licking mayonnaise from the side of the jar when he spotted me.

"So hungry . . . ," he murmured — in my voice! "So hungry! I haven't eaten in over two hundred years!"

He dropped the jar to the floor and stared down at me.

I let out a cry when I saw his eyes.

He had my face, my hair, my whole body.

But the eyes were dead and blank. I stared up into two deep, dark holes. Holes as black as death.

He bit off the top of a carton of buttermilk and tilted the carton over his mouth. Buttermilk ran down his chin and puddled at his feet.

"I know who you are," he gurgled. "You're wasting your time."

I stared up at him, stared into those deep holes where my eyes used to be.

A sick grin spread over his face. "Want to know who I am?" he asked. "I'm *you.*"

"No! I want my body back!" I cried.

The words came out in cat yowls. But he seemed to understand me.

"Go back to the graveyard," he said through clenched teeth. "That's your home now. You're a graveyard ghoul."

"No —" I choked out. "Give me my body back."

"Ha." The ghoul laughed. "You call this a body? This scrawny collection of bones! I don't want this body."

He ripped the glasses from his face. Threw them to the floor and stomped on them.

"My glasses!" I screamed. "You didn't have to do that!"

"As soon as I finish eating, know what else I'm going to do?" he leered. "I'm going to go out and find another body — a good, strong body — and I'm going to *destroy* yours!"

"Noooo!" I screamed. I leaped at him. I landed on his leg — and clung to it with all four paws.

I'm going back in, I decided. I'm taking my body back. But he grabbed me roughly by the back of the neck. And pulled me up in front of his sneering face.

"Did you think it was going to be that easy?" he smirked. "Don't you know who you're dealing with, kitty cat? I'm Oswald Manse. What chance do you have against me?"

Holding me in front of him, the ghoul tightened his hand on the back of my neck.

Tightened . . . tightened . . .

"Please —" I murmured with my last breath. "Please —"

22

ain shot through my body as the ghoul tightened his grasp on my throat. My fur bristled in panic.

A door swung open in front of me. We were halfway down the basement steps before I realized what was happening.

He carried me across the dark basement, to a corner behind the furnace. Holding me with one hand, he rustled something on the floor.

I couldn't see it. But the sound sent a chill of fear down my back. I kicked hard with all four legs. But I couldn't kick free.

And then, without warning, he let go.

I fell hard, into darkness. Darkness on all four sides.

Blinking, I climbed to my feet. And realized he had dropped me into a cardboard carton.

The lid slammed shut over my head.

I let out a yowl.

The carton shook as he kicked it. I toppled onto my side.

"Don't cry, kitty," I heard him say as he walked away. "You tried your best. But you lost."

I stood in the carton, listening to the ghoul's footsteps stomp up the stairs. I heard the basement door close behind him.

I haven't lost yet! I told myself.

I clawed the side of the box.

I tried to chew it with my teeth.

Then I tried clawing again, slashing at it until my nails ached and throbbed.

This isn't going to work, I realized. I stared at the top of the carton. I tried pushing my head against the side.

I can't escape, I decided. I'm too small. I'm not strong enough.

I lowered my head sadly.

And felt something drop onto my back.

It prickled as it walked across my fur.

"Ohhhhh." I let out a terrified moan.

I didn't have to see it. I knew what it was.

A spider.

I raised a paw and batted the spider off my fur. It landed in front of me on the floor of the carton.

Its legs scratched the cardboard as it moved, sending chills down my back.

Oh, please, I thought. Why do I have to be trapped in here with a *spider*?

It crawled steadily toward me.

Closer . . . closer.

I — I can't take this, I thought.

I raised a paw.

I took a deep breath and started to bring it down on top of the spider.

I'll squash it, I decided. I have to squash it.

My paw was nearly down to the carton floor when something made me stop.

An idea. An inspiration!

Whoa! Good thing I didn't kill it, I told myself. The spider is my way out of here!

I rested my paw carefully, lightly, on top of the spider. And I concentrated . . . concentrated . . .

I felt myself floating into darkness. Floating into a tight, dark space.

Yes.

Inside the spider now.

I tested the legs. Took several spidery breaths. I felt light. I felt strong.

I'll never be afraid of spiders again, I realized. Because now I *am* one!

I slid through the crack in the carton and began the long, long walk across the basement.

How long did it take to climb up to my brother's room?

I don't know, but it seemed to take forever.

By the time I made my way across Jason's bedroom floor, my whole body pulsed and throbbed. I wanted to spin a web and disappear inside it for a long rest.

But I forced myself to keep going. Using my last ounce of strength, I dragged myself up his bedspread until I stood on his shoulder.

Jason slept soundly on his side, his mouth slightly open, his curly dark hair matted against the pillow.

"I'm sorry about this, Jason," I said silently. "But I need your body. I would never do this to my own brother if it wasn't a total emergency."

I scuttled onto his cheek. It felt warm and soft under my hairy spider body.

I pressed myself against his skin and concentrated . . . concentrated . . .

In a few seconds, I felt myself slipping down, down into darkness.

Jason didn't move.

He didn't wake up.

I'll give you back your body, I promised silently. As soon as I've captured my own body back, I'll return this one to you.

I sat up. Brushed back the curly dark hair. Opened Jason's eyes.

"Wow," I uttered. A human word. In Jason's voice.

"I'm human again!"

I jumped out of bed — and nearly crashed into the wall.

Jason's body was so heavy.

Be careful, Spencer, I warned myself. You were just a tiny spider. Take your time. Get used to this big, human body.

But, no.

No time to get used to it, I realized. The ghoul said he was going to find a new body — and destroy mine!

I may already be too late.

I ran from the bedroom and raced down the hall. "Mom! Dad!" I cried. "Help me! Mom! Dad!"

I stopped halfway down the hall — as a scream of horror rose up from the kitchen.

I lurched down the stairs, stumbling, carrying my new, heavy body like a big sack of flour. I stopped in the kitchen doorway.

Mom and Dad stood bathed in the light from the open refrigerator door. Their faces were twisted in horror and shock. Their mouths hung open as they saw all the spilled food, broken glass, empty jars and bottles.

"Oh, wow," I murmured.

Mom turned to me. "Jason — who did this?"

"I have to tell you —" I started to explain.

"Who did this? Who? Have you seen Spencer?" Mom demanded.

"*I'm* Spencer!" I declared. "I had to borrow Jason's body."

"Jason — this is no time for jokes!" Dad cried angrily. "Look at this horrible mess!"

"I'm not joking!" I insisted. "You've *got* to listen to me! I'm Spencer. A ghoul stole my body. So I had to take Jason's body. I —"

"Not now, Jason," Mom interrupted. She turned to Dad. "I told Spencer not to let him watch any more monster movies."

"You've got to listen to me!" I shrieked at the top of Jason's lungs. *"I have to get my body back before the ghoul destroys it. I need your help!"*

"Go to your room," Dad snapped. He waved me to the steps. "Go. Now. We'll talk later. Mom and I have a big cleanup on our hands. Someone must have broken into the house."

"But — but — but —" I sputtered.

I could see they weren't going to listen. So I turned and ran upstairs.

I pulled on a pair of jeans and a sweatshirt. Then I grabbed Jason's parka and raced out the front door.

Someone has got to listen to me! I told myself. Someone has got to do something.

I ran to the corner and stopped with a gasp. My shoes crunched over broken glass.

Two cars parked at the curb had their windshields shattered. The hoods and trunks were bent and battered, as if someone had taken a sledgehammer to them.

I trotted past, staring up at the houses and garages. Flames rose out of a car in the next driveway. Garbage cans were overturned.

The door to the next house stood wide open. I heard a baby crying inside.

The front windows of the house after that were shattered. Bright orange flames blazed from the curtains.

On the corner, flames shot out of a mailbox. Two more cars were battered, their windshields smashed to tiny shards of glass.

From down the street, I heard angry cries and frightened shrieks. Shrill wails of panic filled the air. I saw people running in bathrobes and paja-mas.

At the end of the block, the woods were on fire. I saw a van on its side, tires slashed. Heavy black smoke made me choke and cover my eyes.

Squinting through the smoke, I saw the ghoul. A shadowy figure moving through the flames, moving from house to house, destroying every-thing in his path.

In the distance, I heard the rise and fall of sirens. Sirens on all sides. Fire engines . . . The po-lice.

This is all my fault, I thought, gripped with hor-ror. All my fault. I knocked over that double grave-stone. I gave him a way out of the graveyard.

The ghoul darted across the street. He rocked a car until he tilted it onto its side. His high, shrill laughter rose over the screams of horror from people in their houses.

All my fault . . . all my fault . . .

The words repeated in my mind.

And then I saw me — my body — charge up to a fireman who was fighting one of the blazes. The ghoul reached out and snatched an ax from his hand.

"Hey! Give that back to me!" The fireman bolted forward to grab it back. But the ghoul swung it wildly at him. The fireman backed off.

The ghoul dashed down the street and swung the ax at a mailbox post.

The post snapped in two. The mailbox clattered to the street.

He charged up to a garage and began chopping away at the garage door. Splintering it. Swinging again.

And then I heard a fierce cry: "Drop that ax!"

I spun around and saw two dark-uniformed police officers, their faces grim, their eyes reflecting the flames of the house next door.

"Drop the ax!" the officer repeated. He had a hand on his gun holster.

The ghoul in my body whirled around. The dark, empty eyes glared at the two policemen. And then he swung the ax, swung the ax at an officer's head.

"Drop it — or we'll shoot!" the officer boomed.

"No!" I cried, hurtling over to them. "No! Don't shoot! That's my body!"

"Get away, kid!" an officer yelled.
The ghoul swung the ax again.
"Don't shoot him!" I screamed.
"We have no choice!" the policeman cried.
I froze in horror as they raised their guns.

25

"Nooo!" I wailed. "That's my body! It's mine! Don't destroy it!"

Both officers turned to me.

"Are you crazy, kid?"

"Get away from here — now!"

The officers and I turned back to the ghoul.

He had vanished.

I lowered my hands to my knees and struggled to catch my breath. The two officers took off to search for the ghoul.

I heard screams over the fence, coming from the next yard. Frank Foreman's yard. I leaped over the fence and saw the ghoul demolishing the Foremans' toolshed with the ax.

I ducked behind a tree and watched him, trying

to figure out the best way to get my body back from him.

In seconds the shed sat in splinters. "Hmmmm," the ghoul murmured. "Firewood."

Then before I could cry out, the ghoul lit a match and set the pile ablaze.

The dry wood shot up in flames instantly.

The ghoul stared deep into the fire, the flames reflecting in the dark holes that were once my eyes.

The fire blazed up, with flames leaping to the branches of a nearby tree. A tree that hung directly over the Foremans' house!

Oh, no! The Foremans' house is going to catch on fire! I realized. I'd better go in and warn them!

As I darted from my hiding spot, Frank Foreman charged out his back door.

"What are you doing?" he screamed at the ghoul in my body. "Spencer, I'm going to kill you!"

The ghoul whirled around.

He studied Frank. Then he smiled his evil smile. "Now, *that* kid has a good body. Strong, muscular. That's the body for Oswald Manse!"

Frank bolted across the backyard. "I'm going to pound you into the ground, Spencer! But first I'm going to break every bone in your body!"

"NO!" I ran in front of Frank to block him. "Call the police! Call the fire department. Get help!"

As I argued with Frank, the fire spread across

the lawn. I could feel the heat through my sneakers.

Then with a sudden burst, flames shot up in front of us.

"Whoa!" Frank leaped away.

"I know who you are." The ghoul grabbed my jacket and jerked me away from the flames. "I'm going to take over Frank's body," he whispered in my ear. "Then I'm going to throw *your* body into the flames — and we'll watch it burn."

26

The fire roared in front of us.

The wood planks of the shed crackled in the scorching blaze.

The ghoul stepped up to the fire. He reached his arms out to the leaping flames. "Want to watch your hands burn?" he sneered. "Say good-bye to your fingers, Spencer!"

"Noooo!" I screamed. I grabbed the ghoul's arm and jerked him back.

"You're sick!" Frank tackled the ghoul. He pinned his shoulders to the ground. "Jason." He turned to me. "I'll hold him here. Get your parents!"

I started for help — but stopped when I heard Frank moan. "My head — it hurts. It hurts so much!"

"Let him go!" I lunged for Frank and pulled him off the ghoul. "He's trying to steal your body!"

"You're as crazy as your brother!" Frank jerked away from me. "I'm calling the cops!" He charged out of the backyard.

The ghoul chased after him — but stopped when he saw Frank wave down a police car.

I watched the ghoul turn quickly, jump over some bushes, and disappear from sight.

I have to get my body back. But how? I asked myself. I need some help. But no one will believe me. No one will listen to me.

"Whoa," I murmured out loud. A face flashed into my mind. Audra's face.

Audra was with me in the graveyard. She saw me tilt over that double gravestone. She saw Frank and his pals tie me to a grave.

Maybe Audra will listen to me, I thought. Maybe Audra will believe me.

If there are two of us, people will have to listen.

Audra is my last hope . . . my last hope.

I raced down the street. Past burning houses and screaming people.

Audra's block was bathed in darkness. The ghoul hadn't reached it — yet.

I sprinted up the steps to Audra's house.

I peered into the front window. No lights on. Everyone must be asleep.

I ran around to the back of the house. Audra's bedroom faced the yard.

I gazed into her window. I could see her inside, covers pulled up to her chin, sleeping peacefully on her back, her long black hair spread over the pillow.

"Audra," I called softly. "Audra, wake up."

She couldn't hear me.

I knocked on the window. She lifted her head off the pillow and squinted at me.

"Let me in. Please."

Audra slipped out of bed. She pushed open the window, and I climbed inside.

"Audra — it's me, Spencer," I choked out, frantic to tell her my story, frantic for her to believe me. "I know I look like Jason. I had to borrow Jason's body. You see — the ghouls escaped. I mean —"

She rubbed her sleepy eyes. "Jason, you're not making any sense."

"I'm not Jason! I'm Spencer!" I cried. "A ghoul stole my body! You've got to believe me! You've got to help me!"

"You're crazy." Audra's voice trembled. She took a step back.

She reached behind her and clicked on a table lamp. Light flooded the room.

"Please! You have to help me!" I gazed pleadingly into her eyes.

Her eyes.

Not pale green eyes flecked with gold.

No irises . . . no irises at all.

Just holes in the center of Audra's eyes. Deep black holes.

I stared into the gaping black hollows that were once Audra's beautiful eyes. "I know the truth. You're a ghoul!" I cried. "You've taken over Audra's body."

And then I remembered the faint voice I heard in the cemetery. The voice calling to me: "Help me. Help me . . . please."

"Audra is trapped up in the cemetery! Isn't she?" I shouted. "She's up there now. That was Audra calling me. Wasn't it?"

"That doesn't matter anymore. Does it?" The ghoul grinned at me. "It's Audra's turn to stay in the graveyard. And it's my chance to be alive!"

"Nooooo!" A hoarse cry of protest burst from my throat. I dove for the window.

But two strong hands seized my shoulders — and yanked me back into the room. "Sorry," the ghoul whispered. "I can't let you go. I'm never going back to that grave again. I don't want to be Martin Manse anymore. I'm Audra now!"

"Martin Manse!" I gasped.

"Yes!" The ghoul spun me around.

I watched in horror as the black circles of his eyes turned to liquid. Spread like pools of ink. Filled up his eyes. Filled them — until the whites were completely gone.

The ghoul inhaled deeply. Then, grabbing my waist, he lifted me off my feet — and hurled me across the room.

"Ohhhh." I uttered a groan of pain as my head slammed hard against the wall.

I crumbled to the floor.

The world tilted away . . . tilted away . . .

I saw a flash of bright red . . . blood-red . . . and then everything faded . . . faded to black.

28

Pain throbbed through my head, down my neck.

I struggled to open my eyes.

A knock on the bedroom door snapped me alert.

"Audra — what was that noise?" her mother called from the hall. "I heard a loud thud."

The door swung open.

The ghoul rushed toward Audra's mother. "Would you believe it, Mom? I fell out of bed."

"Are you okay?" her mother asked her.

This is my chance, I thought.

Shaking off the pain, I pulled myself to my feet. I lurched out the window.

I could hear their startled cries behind me.

I glanced back once to see if the ghoul was following me. I didn't see him, so I took off.

I raced up the steep slope of Highgrave Hill.

The grass was slick and wet with early morning dew. The moon was fading in a brightening sky.

Below me, I heard the wail of sirens. I could see walls of flame.

Black smoke choked the sky.

Gasping, my heart throbbing in my chest, I ran up to the graveyard gate.

I have to find Audra. Together we'll beat those two ghouls. We'll get our bodies back, I thought. I know we can do this together!

I burst through the gate — and stopped.

The graveyard ghouls hovered over their tombstones. "Bodies. Bodies," they moaned. "We want bodies too."

A boy about my age floated toward me. The skin on one of his cheeks hung loosely off the bone. "I want your body," he rasped.

"No!" an old woman cried. "His body is mine!"

"I want your body," the other ghouls moved in.

They formed a circle around me. Joined their bony hands. And began their eerie dance. "I want your body," they chanted as their legs shuffled stiffly.

I suddenly felt dizzy.

My legs weakened. I couldn't move.

Their dance of death held me in a trance.

"Stop!" I cried. "Don't do this to me!"

"You're a ghoul," the boy rasped. "You're just like us. You're a graveyard ghoul!"

"NO!" I cried. And with a burst of energy I broke free from their spell.

I charged through the circle. "Audra?" I shouted. "Are you here? Audra?"

Silence.

"Audra?" I called, running through the rows of graves. "Audra? It's me! I —"

"Jason?" I heard her voice, soft and weak. "Over here. Under the big willow tree."

I turned and charged toward the voice.

And stumbled over a gravestone.

It toppled to the ground with a heavy *THUD*, and I fell on top of it.

"Oh, no. Not another one," I muttered.

I started to scramble to my feet. In the fading moonlight, the words engraved on the stone caught my eye: DEFEAT DEATH ONLY BY LIVING.

What does *that* mean? I wondered.

I stood up, pulling dead leaves from my hair.

"Jason — over here!" Audra's weak cry.

"It's me — Spencer!" I called to her. "I had to borrow Jason's body. Where are you, Audra?"

"Right here. Next to you. But I can't figure out how to move. I — I feel like air."

"I'll help you," I said. "I'll get you out of here."

"How?" she asked.

"Uh . . ." I swallowed hard. "Well . . ."

And then I heard a noise from the graveyard gate.

I turned toward the sound. And saw a large black dog, a black Lab, come loping into the cemetery.

He wandered toward us, head bent, sniffing graves along the way.

"Yes!" I cried happily. "A dog!"

"So what?" Audra whispered.

"You can slip into his body," I told her.

"Huh? How?"

"You just have to concentrate," I told her. "You can use the dog's body to take you to town. Then maybe . . . maybe, we can get our own bodies back."

My voice trailed off.

It was a *big* maybe.

"Can I really take over the dog?" Audra asked in a tiny voice.

"You have to," I replied. "And we have to hurry — before the ghouls get this body too."

I reached out my hand to pet the dog, to keep him calm while Audra slipped into his body.

"Nice dog. Nice boy," I repeated softly.

He raised his smooth black head.

Gazed up at me.

Then spun around and loped away.

106

29

"Get him!" Audra cried.

The dog trotted toward the gate. I started after him.

I stopped when I spotted something white poking up from the dirt. A bone?

I stopped and yanked it out of the ground.

Yes. A bone.

A human bone? The thought made me shudder.

I let out a long, loud whistle.

The dog stopped. He turned and gazed at me.

I waved the bone in the air — and he came trotting back. I held it out to him and let him sniff it.

"Quick, Audra! Do it now!" I whispered. "Slip into his body!"

"I — I don't know how," Audra wailed. "How do I turn into a dog? It's impossible!"

"Just concentrate. Concentrate on moving into him — and you'll do it. You'll see."

I waited for Audra to make her move.

The dog licked at the bone.

"Hurry, Audra."

The dog ran his big, wet tongue over my fingers.

"Audra, where are you?" I whispered.

"I'm here. Concentrating."

"You've got to hurry."

"I'm trying!" Audra cried. "I'm trying as hard as I can. But it's not working."

"Think, Audra! Just think about slipping into him!" I urged.

The dog rubbed his head against my arm. He unfurled his tongue again and licked my wrist. Then — suddenly — his body stiffened. He chomped down hard on my hand.

"Owwww!" I let out a sharp cry and jerked my hand away.

The dog growled. He shook his body back and forth, as if fighting an invisible enemy.

"That's it, Audra! You're doing it! Don't give up!" I cried.

The dog twisted furiously. He fell to the ground and rolled over and over. He kicked out his legs. Growled fiercely. Then his body went limp.

"Audra — are you in there?" I stared at the unmoving dog.

He opened his mouth in a soft *YIP* — and I

knew Audra had made the move. She was in the dog's body.

"Yes!" I shouted. "Let's go!"

We tore through the cemetery. And raced down Highgrave Hill.

The sky was turning morning pink. A red sun hung low, rising over town.

As we neared the bottom of the hill, we heard the screams. The cries for help. The sirens.

Police cars, fire engines, and ambulances choked the streets.

Flames shot out of houses and store windows.

Black smoke billowed up from the burning buildings.

"Look!" I pointed to a house totally destroyed by flames. It was Frank Foreman's house. He stood outside with his family. They huddled together, staring in disbelief at the ruins.

I felt sorry for him.

I felt sorry for everyone.

I turned to Audra, loping beside me. "What are we going to do?" I asked. "What can we possibly do?"

30

We ran through the streets, through a trail of destruction. My jaw dropped as I gawked at the wreckage.

Street signs lay scattered on the ground, hacked off at the tops. Pay phones had been ripped free from their wiring. The phone booths lay shattered on their sides.

Windows were smashed. Shards of glass carpeted the streets.

I ran by an overturned car parked on someone's lawn. As I passed it, it burst into flames.

We turned onto my block — and I cried out in surprise. "There they are!"

Audra and Spencer. Our bodies! Axes in hand. Running side by side up my front lawn.

"Come on, Audra!" I cried in panic. "They're going to wreck my house!"

The Spencer ghoul raised his ax and smashed through our front door. The Audra ghoul heaved his ax through the living room window.

I heard shrill screams inside. Remy and Charlotte's screams.

Through the smashed window, I could see them holding each other in the center of the room.

"Jason, help us!" Remy spotted me outside and cried out in fear. "Spencer has gone crazy!"

I saw Mom and Dad rush in from the kitchen. They pulled Remy and Charlotte away from the window.

The two ghouls leaped through the broken window.

Audra and I charged in after them.

I had no plan. I didn't know how to fight the ghouls. I just knew I had to stop them from hurting my family.

"Spencer! What's *wrong* with you? Give me that ax right now!" Dad was screaming at the ghoul.

Mom let out a terrified shriek as the ghouls raised their axes in the air.

"Noooo!" I wailed, diving toward them.

"Jason! Run!" Mom pleaded with me. "Go get help!"

Audra, inside the black Lab, lowered her head and let out a low, menacing growl. Then she barked ferociously at the ghouls.

The two ghouls spun around to face us.

I took a deep breath. "Go back to the cemetery

where you belong!" I screamed. "Give us back our bodies, and go back to your graves!"

The two ghouls grinned at each other.

"Spencer! Audra! What's *wrong* with you?" Dad cried. "Put down the axes — and let's talk!"

"Dad — *I'm* Spencer!" I said. "I tried to tell you. These aren't Spencer and Audra. They're Oswald and Martin Manse. They're ghouls!"

Mom and Dad exchanged confused glances. Remy and Charlotte pressed their backs against the wall.

"Get *out* of here!" I screamed at the ghouls.

The Spencer ghoul let out a furious cry. He swung his ax down on the coffee table and split it in two.

Remy and Charlotte burst into tears. Mom and Dad, mouths open in horror, stepped back to protect them.

Laughing, the two ghouls raised their axes and chopped at our piano.

I stood helplessly, thinking hard, frantically trying to come up with a way to stop them.

With a fierce growl, Audra leaped to the attack.

She dove at the ghoul in my body — and sank her teeth into his leg.

He cried out in surprise. The ax fell from his hands.

Snarling, Audra bit into the leg.

The ghoul twisted and turned. He thrashed his arms wildly, tilting back his head in a howl of pain.

As he struggled, the Audra ghoul menaced my family, holding the ax high in front of him. "The dead shall live, and the living shall die!" he proclaimed.

"Audra — wh-what are you *saying*?" Mom stammered. "Please — s-stop this!"

"We don't understand!" Dad cried. "What do you kids want? Why are you doing this?"

The Spencer ghoul uttered an angry cry. He kicked hard and freed his leg from Audra's teeth. Then he bent down — picked up the black Lab, and heaved it against the wall.

The Audra ghoul handed him his ax. Then their eyes narrowed coldly as they turned to me.

"Get him," the Spencer ghoul said through gritted teeth.

31

"Ohhhh." Uttering a low cry, I turned and bolted out of the house.

The two ghouls lumbered after me. "Don't let him get away," the Spencer ghoul growled.

I ran down the front lawn.

Heavy gray clouds covered the morning sun. I could hear sirens in the distance.

"Give me back my body!"

Who said that? The shrill cry made me stop.

I glanced around, but I didn't see anyone.

"Give me back my body," the voice repeated, so close, from right next to me.

"Jason? Is that you?" I choked out.

"Yes. I want my body back."

The two ghouls raised their axes as they closed in on me.

"Not now!" I cried. "Jason — please! Not now!"

"Yes — now!" he insisted. "I need my body. I'm taking it back!"

"Jason — *not now*!" I screeched.

The ghouls stepped closer.

And I felt something heavy pushing down on my head.

Jason!

Pushing down, down on me.

"ason — *please!*" I gasped.

But he pressed down heavily.

I tried to fight back. Concentrated . . . concentrated . . .

But my right arm started to pump up and down. Jason had taken over one arm.

And then my left leg started to bend. It kicked hard.

"Jason — stop!" I begged.

He had taken over half the body.

I swung my arm. Bobbed the head up and down. Bent and twisted, trying to toss him out. Trying to take back control.

"Jason . . ."

I could feel myself growing weaker. Feel him moving in, taking command.

I glanced up to see the ghouls stop and stare.

Their black eyes bulged wide, watching Jason and me struggle.

I swung one arm. I dragged a leg. I tried to move away.

Jason fought back, moving his leg.

As we struggled, the body did a strange dance.

Neighbors stared. My family watched in shock and horror from the front steps.

I hip-hopped over the grass, swinging one arm.

Jason made the body hop back. Then skip.

A wild dance. A frantic dance.

And suddenly, I heard a groan of pain.

I looked up to see the ghouls shut their eyes. They both opened their mouths in long, low groans.

They clutched their stomachs.

What is happening? I wondered.

Jason and I continued our wild dance, struggling for control of the body. Flapping our arms, bending our knees, hopping and skipping in a desperate rhythm.

And to my shock, both ghouls dropped weakly to their knees on the grass.

The axes fell from their hands. They rolled their eyes and uttered faint moans.

I kicked and tossed an arm.

The two ghouls groaned again.

It's the dance, I realized. The crazy dance.

The dance is making them weak.

And then the strange words on the gravestone returned to me. The words I hadn't understood.

DEFEAT DEATH ONLY BY LIVING.

What is a better sign of being alive than *dancing*? I asked myself.

Yes. Dancing. When people dance, it means they're really alive!

I did it! I figured out how to defeat Oswald Manse!

I had always *hated* dancing. I *never* danced.

But now I knew I had to dance and dance — and never stop!

"I'm going to get my body back!" I shouted at the ghoul.

"It's *my* body now!" the ghoul moaned. "No one beats Oswald Manse! No one!"

I kicked my legs. And waved my hands. I snapped my fingers and moved my body in a wild, frantic rhythm.

"Stop!" the ghoul clutched his chest in agony. "It's *my* body now. . . ."

I grabbed the black Lab by the front paws. Pulled her up on her hind legs. And danced with her.

Danced . . . danced . . .

Until, moaning and crying, the two ghouls shut their eyes and collapsed to the grass.

Yes!

We defeated them!

"We did it, Audra!" I cried, letting go of her paws. "We did it!"

I wanted to shout and laugh and sing. I wanted to dance until I couldn't dance anymore.

But then I turned to my body and Audra's body — and my heart sank.

They lay facedown, arms and legs sprawled over the grass.

Lifeless.

So totally lifeless.

Too late, I thought.

Too late to slip back in.

Audra and I are doomed.

No bodies. We'll be shadows too.

Nothing but shadows . . . forever.

taring at my lifeless body on the grass, I
floated out of Jason's body.

He instantly took charge. I watched him test his
hands, bend his knees, open and close his mouth.

"I'm *me*!" he declared happily.

But would I ever be *me* again?

"Come on, Audra," I urged the dog. "Hurry.
Maybe we're not too late. Maybe we can be our-
selves again. Maybe we can do it."

The dog trotted beside me.

I floated up over my body.

Please . . . please! I prayed. Let me back in.

I concentrated. Concentrated . . .

Felt myself slipping down, down . . .

Down into a deep darkness.

I opened my eyes.

I saw the clouds roll away. Bright sunlight beamed down on us, spreading over the lawn.

"We made it, Audra! We made it back just in time!" I shouted.

I felt so happy, I jumped up and down. I spun in a circle — and let my skirt twirl around me.

Huh?

I glanced down — at my purple skirt, my purple tights, my silky black blouse, my bright blue nail polish!

I touched my head and ran my hands through my long, silky black hair.

"Whoooa!" I turned to Audra — but Audra wasn't there beside me.

I was staring at *myself*!

"Uh . . . Audra," I said, tossing back my black hair. "I think we made a little mistake. What do we do *now*?"

About R.L. Stine

R.L. Stine is the most popular author in America. He is the creator of the *Goosebumps*, *Give Yourself Goosebumps*, *Fear Street*, and *Ghosts of Fear Street* series, among other popular books. He has written over 200 scary novels for kids. Bob lives in New York City with his wife, Jane, teenage son, Matt, and dog, Nadine.

Welcome to the new millennium of fear

Check out this
chilling preview of
what's next from
R.L. STINE

Brain Juice

2

"**A**nd that's why you came to see me?" Uncle Frank asked, leaning forward in his chair. His eyes moved from Nathan to Lindy. "Because you think you're stupid?"

"Yes," Nathan agreed, pushing his glasses up on his nose.

He and Lindy hadn't touched the brownies and milk their aunt Jenny had brought in. They both sat stiffly in chairs across from Uncle Frank, their hands clasped tightly in their laps.

"Maybe we're not really stupid," Lindy chimed in. "But we're not really smart, either."

"We're not smart *enough*," Nathan said.

Uncle Frank cleared his throat. He narrowed his eyes thoughtfully. "And what do you want me to do?"

"Well . . ." Nathan hesitated.

"You're the smartest person in our family," Lindy spoke up. "And you're a scientist, right?"

Uncle Frank nodded.

"And you do scientific work about the brain, right?" Nathan added.

Uncle Frank nodded again.

"So . . ." Nathan continued. "We thought maybe you knew some way Lindy and I could get smarter."

"Isn't there *anything* you can do?" Lindy pleaded. "Any way at all to make us smarter?"

Uncle Frank rubbed his chin. "Yes," he replied finally. "Yes, I do have something that might work."

"What *is* it?" Nathan and Lindy asked in unison.

ncle Frank leaned forward in his
chair. He started to reply — but suddenly swung around and stared at the doorway to
the kitchen.

"What's wrong?" Nathan asked.

Uncle Frank turned back to them. "Did you
hear something? Probably just Jenny." He shook
his head. "Funny. I've had the strangest feeling
that I'm being watched."

"Weird," Lindy muttered, glancing to the doorway. She didn't see anything unusual there.

Uncle Frank shrugged. "I guess all scientists
have that feeling when they're working on something top secret." He tugged down the sleeves of
his white sweatshirt. He seemed to be thinking
hard about something.

"So . . . do you really think you can help us?" Lindy asked eagerly.

"Yes. Yes, I do," her uncle replied after a long moment.

Nathan slapped the arms of the chair excitedly. "You mean it? Something to make us smarter?" he asked.

Uncle Frank nodded. "Yes. I have been working on something. But . . ." He glanced to the doorway again. "It's very top secret. And very dangerous."

Nathan gasped. Lindy swallowed hard.

"I don't know. Maybe it's too dangerous," Uncle Frank said softly.

"But — if it will work . . . ?" Nathan urged.

"Oh, it will work," the scientist replied. "It will definitely work. I've tested it out. I wouldn't even try it on you if I hadn't tested it out."

"So . . . can we try it?" Lindy asked.

"Can we?" Nathan cried.

Uncle Frank frowned. Once again, he seemed lost in thought.

Then he startled the kids by jumping quickly to his feet. "Okay!" he declared enthusiastically. "Okay. Okay. Let's try it."

The scientist left the kids in the living room. Humming to himself, he disappeared into his lab. A few minutes later, still humming, he made his way into the kitchen.

Jenny looked up from the kitchen table where she was writing a grocery list on a long pad. She was a pretty, blond-haired woman, with soft brown eyes and a warm smile. "What's up, Frank? Did you and the kids finish your top secret, private talk? Can I go out and see them now?"

He motioned for her to sit still. "Poor kids," he muttered. He opened a food cabinet and began rummaging through bottles and jars.

Jenny came up beside him at the kitchen counter. "What's wrong? Why did they come to see you?"

Frank grunted as he found what he was searching for. He pulled out a small bottle of purple grape juice.

Then he turned to his wife. "Nathan and Lindy somehow got it into their heads that they're not smart."

Jenny raised her eyes from the grape juice to her husband. "Excuse me? Not smart?"

Dr. King nodded. He examined the purple bottle. "The two of them are really upset. They came to ask me if I had anything to make them smarter."

Jenny's mouth dropped open. "And what did you tell them? I hope you told them that they are both *very* smart. That they shouldn't worry about —"

He raised a finger to his lips. "I'm going to do

something to build up their confidence," he whispered. "That's their whole problem. They have no confidence. They don't believe in themselves."

"What are you going to do?" his wife asked suspiciously.

"I think this will do the trick," the scientist replied. "I went into the lab and made a label of my own on the computer."

Dr. King set the grape juice bottle on its side on the counter. Then he held up the label he had printed:

BRAIN JUICE.

Jenny frowned at the label. "What on earth is Brain Juice?"

Dr. King chuckled. "I'm going to tell them it's a secret formula that will make them smarter. You'll see. It's only grape juice, of course. But it really will help them. If they *believe* they are smart, they really will be smart."

Jenny sighed. "Worth a try, I guess." She hurried to the living room to talk to the kids.

Dr. King turned back to the bottle. He carefully stuck the BRAIN JUICE label over the grape juice label. Then he turned the bottle in his hand, making sure that the grape juice label didn't show through.

"Perfect," he declared to himself. "Perfect. You can't see the old label at all. It's now a bottle of Brain Juice."

Pleased with his clever idea, Dr. King smiled to

himself. Still admiring the bottle, he started to the living room with it.

The phone rang. The phone in his lab down the hall.

He set the bottle down on the counter beside the pantry door and hurried to the lab to answer it.

As soon as the kitchen stood empty, the two aliens squeezed out of their hiding place. They bounced out of the pantry, leaving a wet stain on the floor behind them.

"Our chance, but we must hurry," Gobbul whispered, eyeing the doorway.

"Did you see those humans in the other room?" Morggul replied excitedly. "They look young and strong. If we can make them smart enough, they could be the slaves we have come for."

"Perhaps," Gobbul replied. He wrapped a green tentacle around the grape juice bottle. "We shall see. We shall see . . ."

He unscrewed the top of the bottle.

Morggul's body made a wet slapping sound on the floor as he moved closer to his leader. "If we take the children as slaves, I want to eat the scientist. And his mate. I want to eat them alive, while they're still fresh. Food tastes so much better when it's screaming."

Gobbul pushed his partner back. "Stop thinking only of your stomachs," he scolded. "We have work to do."

Morggul made a spitting sound through the purple pods up and down his arms.

Gobbul raised the Brain Juice bottle and poured the grape juice down the sink. Then he pulled another bottle of purple liquid from a pouch in his upper stomach.

Carefully, he poured his own purple liquid into the Brain Juice bottle. "Our only supply of Brain Energizer Fluid," he muttered. "Let's hope it works." He capped the bottle and placed it back on the counter.

"Hurry, Morggul." He gave his fat partner a push with all four tentacles. "Back into the pantry. Before the scientist King returns."

Morggul gazed at the purple bottle. His lower mouth frowned. His upper mouth said, "No human has ever drunk this formula. How do we know what side effects it will have? Maybe it will *kill* them!"

got Brain juice?

Go ahead and try some!
Your brain will never be the same...

GOOSEBUMPS®
SERIES 2000

#12: Brain Juice

In Bookstores this November.

Visit the web site at http://www.scholastic.com/goosebumps

SCHOLASTIC

GBT498

PARACHUTE

PREPARE TO BE SCARED!

Goosebumps
SERIES 2000
R.L. STINE

- BCY39988-8 **#1: Cry of the Cat**
- BCY39990-X **#2: Bride of the Living Dummy**
- BCY39989-6 **#3: Creature Teacher**
- BCY39991-8 **#4: Invasion of the Body Squeezers (Part I)**
- BCY39992-6 **#5: Invasion of the Body Squeezers (Part II)**
- BCY39993-4 **#6: I Am Your Evil Twin**
- BCY39994-2 **#7: Revenge R Us**
- BCY39995-0 **#8: Fright Camp**
- BCY39996-9 **#9: Are You Terrified Yet?**
- BCY76781-X **#10: Headless Halloween**
- BCY76783-6 **#11: Attack of the Graveyard Ghouls**

$3.99 Each!

Available wherever you buy books, or use this order form.

Scholastic Inc., P.O. Box 7502, Jefferson City, MO 65102

Please send me the books I have checked above. I am enclosing $_____ (please add $2.00 to cover shipping and handling). Send check or money order—no cash or C.O.D.s please.

Name _____ Age _____

Address _____

City _____ State/Zip _____

Please allow four to six weeks for delivery. Offer good in the U.S. only. Sorry, mail orders are not available to residents of Canada. Prices subject to change.   GB498

http://www.scholastic.com/goosebumps

SCHOLASTIC   PARACHUTE

Log on for Scares!
Scholastic presents
Goosebumps®
ON THE WEB!
tp://www.scholastic.com/Goosebumps
The latest books!
Start your own Goosebumps reading club!
Author R.L. Stine's tips on writing!
Really gross recipes!
Craft ideas!
How to get Goosebumps stuff: sportswear, CD-ROMs, video releases and more!
Exclusive contests!
Interactive word games and activities!
Parachute Press, Inc. GOOSEBUMPS is a registered trademark of Parachute Press, Inc. All rights reserved.
GWEB1296